ONE GIRL HOLDS
THE FATE OF THE UNIVERSE
IN HER HANDS.

The Melancholy

OF HARUHI SUZUMIYA

First released in Japan in 2003, *The Melancholy of Haruhi Suzumiya* quickly established itself as a publishing phenomenon, drawing much of its inspiration from Japanese pop culture and Japanese comics in particular. With this foundation, the original publication of each book in the Haruhi series included several black-and-white spot illustrations as well as a four-page color insert — all of which are faithfully reproduced here to preserve the authenticity of the first-ever English edition.

NAGARU TANIGAWA

Little, Brown and Company

Hachette Book Group
237 Park Avenue, New York, NY 10017
Visit our Web site at www.lb-teens.com
www.jointhesosbrigade.com

Little, Brown and Company is a division of
Hachette Book Group, Inc.
The Little, Brown name and logo are
trademarks of Hachette Book Group, Inc.

First U.S. Edition: April 2009

Tanigawa, Nagaru.
   [Suzumiya Haruhi no yuutsu. English]
   The melancholy of Haruhi Suzumiya / by Nagaru Tanigawa ; illustrations by
Noizi Ito. —1st U.S. ed.
      p. cm.
   Summary: On the first day at a Japanese high school, an irrepressible
girl announces her lack of interest in "ordinary humans" and proceeds to
form a club dedicated to finding aliens, time travelers, and other forms of
supernatural life, with the intention of having fun with them.
   ISBN 978-0-316-03901-7 (hc) / 987-0-316-03902-4 (pb)
   [1. Supernatural—Fiction. 2. Clubs—Fiction. 3. High schools—Fiction. 4.
Schools—Fiction. 5. Japan—Fiction.] I. Ito, Noizi, ill. II. Title.
PZ7.T16139Me 2009
[Fic]—dc22
                                          2008054396

10 9 8 7 6 5 4 3 2 1

RRD-C

Printed in the United States of America

The Melancholy

OF HARUHI SUZUMIYA

NAGARU TANIGAWA

PROLOGUE

The question of how long someone believed in Santa Claus is a worthless topic that would never come up in idle conversation. Having said that, if you're going to ask me how much of my childhood I spent believing in an old man in a red suit, I can confidently say that I never believed in him to begin with.

I knew that the Santa at the preschool Christmas pageant was just a fake. Digging into my memories, I'm pretty sure that the other kids watching our principal dressed up as Santa didn't think he was real either.

I was a precocious child who didn't need to see Mommy kissing Santa Claus to question the existence of an old man who only worked on Christmas. However, I wouldn't realize that aliens, time travelers, ghosts, demons, espers, and evil organizations and the heroes that battle them in cartoons, monster movies, and comics were made up until some time later.

No, I had probably already realized the truth. I just didn't want to admit it.

Deep in my heart, I wished that aliens, time travelers, ghosts, demons, evil organizations, or espers might just pop up in front of me one day.

Compared to the ordinary world I wake up in every morning, the worlds depicted in cartoons, monster movies, and comics have a certain charm to them.

I wished I could have been born into one of those worlds!

Saving a girl who's been kidnapped by aliens and imprisoned within a huge, transparent pea shell. Repelling a laser-wielding time traveler trying to change history armed only with my courage and wits. Taking out evil spirits and demons with a single incantation. Engaging in psychic battles with espers from a secret organization. Those were the kinds of things I wanted to do!

Wait a minute. Assuming that aliens, etc. were actually to attack, without having any particular special powers, I would have no way to do battle with them. So I did some brainstorming.

A mysterious transfer student suddenly arrives in my class one day. That student turns out to actually be an alien or time traveler or something along those lines with unknown powers. Then, the student happens to be fighting against some evil gang and I just happen to get caught up in that fight. The other student is the main one doing the fighting. I'm just a sidekick. Hey, that sounds cool. Damn, I'm smart.

Or how about this? I'll just go with suddenly waking up one day with special powers — telepathy or psychokinesis or the like. It turns out there are a bunch of other people with special powers. Naturally, there are organizations recruiting such people. Members of a heroic organization come for me and I end up joining them in their battle against evil espers seeking world domination.

However, reality is rather cruel.

Fact is, no one had ever transferred into my class. I'd never seen a UFO. Going to all the local haunted spots yielded nothing in terms of ghosts and demons. Staring intently at the pencil on my desk for two hours didn't even move it a micron. And I'd be more likely to burn a hole in the head of the guy sitting in front of me than to read his mind.

You have to admire how well the laws of physics were written while fighting the urge to laugh at yourself. At some point, I stopped being glued to the TV watching specials on UFOs and stories about psychics. They couldn't possibly exist, though I kind of wished they did. I figured my ability to hold on to my convictions while accepting reality was a sign that I'd matured.

When I graduated from middle school, I also graduated from those childish dreams and became used to the normalcy of the world. Nineteen ninety-nine was my last hope and it wasn't like anything was going to happen that year anyway. We reached the twenty-first century without humankind making it beyond the moon. It looked unlikely that travel to Alpha Centauri and back within a day would happen in my lifetime.

Having pushed such thoughts to the corner of my mind, I entered high school without a care in the world —

And met Haruhi Suzumiya.

CHAPTER 1

My first regret, upon successfully cruising through admission to a local public high school, was that the school was situated atop a rather sizable hill. This meant that I found myself trudging up a winding hill, dripping sweat when it was only spring, feeling like I'd already done enough hiking for a lifetime. The fact that I'd have to embark on this uphill trek every day for the next three years depressed me deeply. Though if I stopped to think for a moment, lying in bed until the last second possible might just be the reason my legs were moving so quickly right then. Which meant that if I were to wake up ten minutes earlier, I'd be able to take a more leisurely pace, and the hike wouldn't be such a pain. Of course, once I factored in how precious those last ten minutes of sleep were, I realized that waking up earlier was simply out of the question. This meant that I would be required to continue the morning workout, which depressed me even more.

And so for the duration of the school commencement ceremony, held in a gratuitously large gymnasium, I, unlike the other new students whose faces shone with hope and anxiety in anticipation of life at a new school, merely looked gloomy. A good number of people from my old middle school were there, and I'd been on pretty good terms with a few of them so I wasn't too concerned about making friends.

It seemed like an odd combination to have guys in blazers and girls in sailor uniforms. Maybe Principal Toupee up on the podium putting everyone to sleep with his droning sound waves happened to be a fan of sailor uniforms? While I was thinking about this, the trite, monotonous commencement suddenly ended, and I shuffled into my assigned classroom, 1-5, with the rest of my classmates, whose faces I would be seeing for the upcoming year, whether I liked it or not.

Okabe, our young homeroom teacher, took the podium with a million-dollar smile he had probably spent an hour practicing in front of the mirror. He then proceeded to inform us that he was a gym teacher, that he was the handball team's advisor, that he played for a handball team back in college which got pretty far in the tournament, that the current school handball team was short on members so you were practically guaranteed a spot as a starter upon joining, and that there was no sport in this world as fun as handball. Having apparently run out of things to say after that long-winded speech, he finished with, "Let's have everyone introduce themselves."

Well, this was the same old way of kicking things off, and I'd expected as much, so it didn't exactly come as a surprise.

Starting from the left side of the seating chart, alternating boy-girl-boy-girl, one by one, people stood up and gave their name, the middle school they went to, and an interesting fact (a hobby, favorite food, etc.) about themselves. Some people just mumbled their way through it. Some people sounded completely relaxed. A few told bad jokes which killed any excitement in the room. And all the while, my turn gradually drew closer. Nerve-racking. You know what I mean, right?

Once I had managed to not stumble over the required autobiography I was practicing in my head, I sat back down in my seat, relishing that liberating feeling you get after taking care of business. In turn, the person behind me stood up — yes, I'll remember this moment for the rest of my life — and spoke the words people would be talking about for years to come.

"Haruhi Suzumiya. From East Middle School."

Everything was still normal at this point. Twisting around to look behind me would have been too much of a hassle, which is why I was facing forward as I listened to her energetic voice.

"I have no interest in ordinary humans. If there are any aliens, time travelers, sliders, or espers here, come join me. That is all."

That made me turn around.

I found a girl with long, straight black hair decorated with a flashy hair band adorning her perfectly proportioned face as she stared back at the gawking students with unusually large, black, determined eyes adorned with long, fringed eyelashes, her soft pink lips tightly pursed.

I was dazzled by Haruhi's snow-white skin. A striking beauty stood before me.

Haruhi let her gaze sweep across the classroom, looking like she was trying to pick a fight, before finally glaring at me, gaping at her with my jaw on the floor, then sat down without so much as cracking a smile.

Is this some kind of a joke?

There were probably big question marks in the minds of everyone in the room as they wondered how they were supposed to react. Are we supposed to laugh?

In hindsight, it was neither a joke nor a laughing matter. Haruhi, no matter when or where, is never joking. She is always dead serious.

I learned this the hard way later on so there's no doubt about it.

Fairies of silence flittered around the classroom for thirty seconds before gym teacher Okabe hesitantly gestured to the next student and the frozen atmosphere finally returned to normal.

And so we met.

I deeply hope that it was mere coincidence.

After capturing the hearts of everyone in the class in every way, Haruhi was relatively quiet for the next few days, playing the role of a seemingly harmless high school girl.

I now understand very well just what people mean by the calm before a storm.

Well, everyone who came to this particular high school was a student with average grades from one of the four city middle schools, which included East Middle School. This meant that some of these students had gone to middle school with Haruhi, so they realized that her decision to stay in the background was probably an omen of some kind. Unfortunately, I didn't know anyone from East Middle, and nobody in the class ever bothered to enlighten me. This led to what happened right after morning homeroom started, a few days after her crazy introduction. This was a moment I'll never forget. I broke the world record for stupidity and spoke to Haruhi Suzumiya.

My domino reaction of misfortune had begun, and I was the one who had knocked the first one down.

But come on. As long as Haruhi Suzumiya sat still with her mouth shut, anyone looking at her would be convinced that she was just a beautiful high school girl. Who's going to blame me for losing my mind for a moment and assuming that I could use the fact that my seat was right in front of hers to approach her?

Naturally, there was only one topic to talk about.

"Hey," I said, as I nonchalantly turned around with a casual smile on my face. "About the stuff in your introduction earlier. How much of it was serious?"

With her arms crossed and her mouth forming an upside-down V, Haruhi stared into my eyes unflinchingly.

"What stuff earlier?"

"Well, you know. The stuff about aliens and whatever."

"Are you an alien?" She asked this with a dead serious look on her face.

"No, but. . . ."

"No, but what?"

". . . Just forget it."

"Don't talk to me then. You're wasting my time."

The tone of her voice and the look she gave me were frigid enough to almost make me apologize out of reflex. Haruhi Suzumiya then stopped staring at me the way one would stare at Brussels sprouts, and with a "hmph," turned to glare in the direction of the blackboard.

Frozen out of a quick response, I was saved by the timely entrance of our homeroom teacher, Okabe.

As I dejectedly turned to face the front of the room, I noticed a number of people looking curiously towards me. When our eyes met, each person would half-smile in a knowing way, as if to say, "Thought so." And then nod as if to offer their condolences.

That kind of left me feeling uncomfortable. It was only later that I learned they had all gone to East Middle.

So yeah. Given that my first contact with Haruhi would probably fall into the "worst ever" category, I had begun wondering if it would be better not to get involved with her. A week went by without anything happening to prove that idea wrong.

However, there were other people in the class who hadn't grasped the situation or were just plain blind to their surroundings. Those classmates would approach Haruhi, who was always in a foul mood, brow wrinkled and mouth looking like an upside-down V, and attempt to start a conversation about one thing or another.

They were just some nosy girls who saw this girl who had isolated herself from day one and wanted to bring her into their circle of friends. I'm sure they were well-intentioned, but you have to take into account who they were dealing with.

"Did you watch that TV show last night? The one that starts at nine."

"No."

"What —? Why not —?"

"Don't care."

"You should try watching an episode. Oh, but you won't know what's going on if you start now. That's right. In that case, I can fill you in on what's happened so far."

"Shut up."

That's how it went.

It'd be one thing if her response had been devoid of emotion, but Haruhi's facial expression and tone of voice were clearly broadcasting irritation, leaving the other person feeling like she'd done something wrong. In the end, all the girl could say was, "Um . . . Well, you know . . ." before slinking away with drooping shoulders. "Did I say something strange?"

Rest assured, you didn't. The only thing strange here is Haruhi's mind.

I don't particularly have a problem with eating alone, but picking at your lunch by yourself while everyone else is chattering at their tables might make people wonder. I'm not saying that's the reason, but when it came time for lunch, I would move my desk next to the tables of Kunikida, someone I'd been relatively close to in middle school, and Taniguchi, a guy from East Middle who happened to sit near me.

That's when the subject of Haruhi Suzumiya came up.

"Hey. You talked to Suzumiya the other day, right?" Taniguchi suddenly asked. "She probably drove you away with some random nonsense."

You got that right.

Taniguchi placed a boiled egg in his mouth and chewed.

"If you're interested in her, I won't mince words. Just let it go. You should be well aware that Suzumiya's a freak."

He mentioned by way of introduction that he'd been in the same class as her for three years in middle school, so he knew what he was talking about.

"She's the strangest girl you'll ever meet. I thought she might calm down after becoming a high school student, but she hasn't changed one bit. You heard her introduction, right?"

"The thing about aliens or whatever?" That was Kunikida, busily picking bones from his grilled fish, cutting in.

"Yep. She said and did a bunch of strange things back in middle school, too. The most famous one would be the graffiti incident on school grounds."

"What's that?"

"There's this machine that uses chalk to draw white lines, right? What was it called again? Whatever. Anyway, someone used that to draw some huge, bizarre pictograph on the school grounds. And whoever it was snuck in at night to do it."

Taniguchi grinned. Maybe he was remembering what had happened?

"You'd be amazed. I arrived at school in the morning to find giant circles and triangles scribbled all over the ground. I couldn't tell what it was supposed to be from up close, so I tried looking at it from the fourth floor. I still couldn't tell what it was supposed to be."

"Oh, I remember seeing that. Wasn't that in the local section of the newspaper? They had an aerial photo. It looked like a failed attempt at a Nazca geoglyph." That was Kunikida. I didn't remember any of this.

"It was. It was. Headlined *Mysterious Graffiti Found on Middle School Grounds.* So it came time to figure out who the culprit behind this ridiculous stunt was."

"And she was the one who did it?"

"She admitted to it, so it had to be her. 'Course, they wanted to know why she did it. They even called her to the principal's office. Seems like all the teachers got together to question her."

"Why'd she do it?"

"Dunno."

With that offhand response, Taniguchi began gulping down his white rice.

"Seems like she never 'fessed up. You try dealing with Suzumiya when she refuses to say a word and gives you that killer glare. Can't do a thing about it. According to one account, the drawing was to invite UFOs. Another said it was a summoning circle for evil demons. Yet another said it was to open a gate to another world. A bunch of rumors popped up, but since she never gave a reason, no one can really say. It's still a mystery."

In my mind, I could picture Haruhi Suzumiya drawing white lines in the pitch-black darkness of the school grounds with an earnest expression on her face. The clattering line marker she's dragging around and the heap of bags of lime were probably taken from the gym storeroom beforehand. She might have at least brought a flashlight. I couldn't help but think that in the flickering light, Haruhi Suzumiya's expression seemed filled with an overwhelming sense of tragic heroism. Only in my imagination, though.

Haruhi Suzumiya was probably genuinely trying to invite UFOs or summon demons or open up a gate to another world. She might have spent the whole night toiling away on the middle school grounds. And then finally, after nothing showed up, she must have been really demoralized.

Just some baseless speculation on my part.

"She also did a bunch of other stuff."

Taniguchi was in the process of finishing off the remaining bits of his lunch.

"One morning, we showed up at the classroom to find all the

desks out in the hall. She drew stars on the roof in paint. She even took a bunch of weird talismans, like the ones they stick on a corpse's head to reanimate it, and stuck them all around school. I really don't get her."

By the way, Haruhi Suzumiya wasn't in the classroom right then. We wouldn't have been able to have this conversation otherwise. Though I got the feeling she wouldn't care, even if she had been there. Speaking of Haruhi Suzumiya, she made a habit of leaving the room the moment fourth period ended and not coming back until right before fifth period started. I'd never seen her bring a lunch so she probably ate in the cafeteria. Still, it can't take an hour to eat lunch. Come to think of it, I could safely say that she was never in the room between classes. I wondered where she wandered off to.

"Even so, she's pretty popular . . ." Taniguchi was still talking. "It's because she has the looks. Plus she's great at sports and probably gets better grades than most. You can't tell she's a freak when she just stands there and keeps her mouth shut."

"Are there any stories about her love life?" That was Kunikida, who hadn't eaten even half as much as Taniguchi.

"For a while, she kept switching from one guy to another. As far as I know, the longest lasted a week, and apparently the shortest was five minutes after she agreed to go out with him. It was always Suzumiya doing the dumping, without exception. She always used the same line. 'I don't have time to deal with ordinary humans!' Then don't agree to go out in the first place!"

Taniguchi was probably speaking from experience. I guess he noticed me looking at him since he hurriedly went on.

"It's just a story I heard. Really. I don't know why, but apparently, she doesn't turn anyone down. Everyone had it figured out by the third year so there wasn't anybody left trying to ask her out. But I get the feeling that the same thing's going to happen in high school. That's why I'm warning you before you get any weird ideas. Give it up. Consider it a friendly warning from a classmate."

There's nothing to give up on. I'm not even interested.

Taniguchi placed his empty lunch box in his bag and smirked.

"If you ask me, then yeah, that's the best one in the class over there. Ryoko Asakura."

Taniguchi stuck his chin toward a cluster of chatting girls with their desks close together. In the center of the cluster with a cheerful smile on her face was Ryoko Asakura.

"As far as I'm concerned, she's gotta be in the top three for our year."

"Did you check out all the freshman girls already or something?"

"Oh, yeah! I assigned them ranks from A to D, and I learned the full names of the ones who ranked A. You only get to live the high school life once. Might as well have fun doing it."

"And Asakura is an A?" Kunikida asked.

"An A+, for sure. Once you've reached my level of expertise, you can tell just by looking at their face. She's definitely a nice person too."

Well, even if you assume that half of Taniguchi's opinionated rambling was a load of bull, Ryoko Asakura was, in fact, a girl who stood out in a different way from Haruhi Suzumiya.

First off, she was a hottie. It was also really sweet how she gave you the feeling she was always smiling. Second, Taniguchi was probably correct in judging that Ryoko was a nice person. By this point, there pretty much wasn't anybody left foolish enough to try to talk to Haruhi Suzumiya. The only human undeterred by the constant rude reception was Ryoko Asakura. She had the temperament of a class president. Third, judging by her responses in class, she seemed to be pretty smart, too. Every question directed toward her was guaranteed to be answered correctly. She was a student any teacher would love to have. Fourth, she was also popular among girls. It had only been a week since school started, and she'd already succeeded in becoming the ringleader of the girls in the class. She definitely had enough charisma to attract the masses.

If you pit her against Haruhi Suzumiya, with her perpetually furrowed brow and incomprehensible thinking pattern, everyone's going to take the former. Myself included, I guess. Either way, they were both way out of Taniguchi's league.

It was still April. At this point, Haruhi Suzumiya had yet to act up. Which meant that for me, it was a month of relaxation. It'd be almost another month before Haruhi started rampaging.

However, I should mention that I was able to gradually observe Haruhi's eccentric behavior during this period.

And so, peculiarity number one.

Her hairstyle changed every day. I noticed a sort of pattern after looking at her for a while. It basically went like this: On Monday, Haruhi would show up with her long, straight hair flowing down her back in a normal fashion. The next day, she would walk in with a ponytail, looking flawless from every angle. *The way it looks so perfect on her is almost more than I can bear.* But then on the next day, she would come to school with her hair tied into two pigtails. The day after that, it would be three. And on Friday, she would have four random spots tied off by ribbons. It was quite an odd sight.

Monday = 0, Tuesday = 1, Wednesday = 2 . . .

In other words, she tied off another part of her hair for every day that passed. After resetting on Monday, she added one per day until Friday. I had no idea what it was supposed to signify. Based on the pattern, she'd eventually end up with six tied-off spots. I wondered what her head looked like on Sunday. I would have liked to see it.

Peculiarity number two. Boys and girls are split up for gym

class so classes 5 and 6 are combined. Girls change in odd-numbered rooms and boys move to even-numbered rooms. Once the class before gym ends, the boys grab their gym clothes and prepare to move to class 6.

As that was happening, Haruhi Suzumiya completely ignored the fact that boys were still present in the classroom and began taking off her uniform.

She would then toss her uniform on her desk and pick up her gym clothes with an indifferent look on her face, as though she viewed the gallery of guys on the same level as pumpkins or potatoes.

At that point, the completely dumbstruck guys, myself included, were kicked out of the room by Ryoko Asakura.

It seems that afterwards, Ryoko led the other girls in lecturing Haruhi, but yeah, it didn't accomplish anything. Haruhi continued to change without giving a damn about her male audience. Which is why when the bell for the break before gym rang, the guys were obligated — per Ryoko's orders — to immediately sprint out of the room.

But damn, she was hot . . . I mean, let's move on.

Peculiarity number three. Haruhi would invariably be absent from the classroom during breaks. And you could count on her to be out the door carrying her bag the second school was out. At first, I thought she went straight home, but apparently not. To my amazement, she had been temporarily joining a wide range of school clubs. You'd see her dribbling around with the basketball team one day only to find her sewing a pillowcase in the handicrafts club the next day and swinging a stick on the lacrosse team the next. She even joined the baseball team, so it didn't look like she was leaving anything out. Every sports club, without exception, fervently pursued her membership. Turning their requests down, she would arbitrarily join a different club every day. In the end, she didn't stick with a single one of them.

What exactly was she trying to accomplish?

Naturally, the rumor that "there's a strange girl in this year's freshman class" spread like wildfire throughout school. It only took about a month before every single person involved with our school knew of Haruhi Suzumiya. By the beginning of May, it reached the point where some people still didn't know the name of the principal, but everybody knew the name Haruhi Suzumiya.

As all of this was going on — well, Haruhi was the only one actually involved — we reached the month of May.

I'm more willing to believe in the chance of someone discovering a plesiosaurus in Lake Biwa than in fate. But if fate does in fact affect the lives of humans from some unknown place, I'm guessing that this was when my wheel of destiny began to turn. I'm positive that someone up there had rewritten my future without my consent.

It was the first day after the Golden Week holidays. I discovered that I had lost track of what day of the week it was as I trudged up the winding hill, dripping sweat in the scorching, abnormal May weather. What was the earth trying to do here? Did it catch yellow fever or something?

"Yo, Kyon."

Someone behind me tapped me on the shoulder. It was Taniguchi.

He had his blazer slung nonchalantly over his shoulder, necktie half-loose, and a grin plastered on his face.

"Did you go somewhere for Golden Week?"

"I took my sister to see our grandmother."

"That's lame."

"What about you?"

"Worked the whole time."

"How is that any better?"

"Kyon, a high school student shouldn't be babysitting his little sister on a merry little trip to visit grandparents. You've gotta act more like a high schooler."

Incidentally, the nickname "Kyon" belongs to me. From what I recall, one of my aunts was the first to call me that. It was a few years back when I hadn't seen her for a while. When she saw me, she went, "Oh, Kyon. You've grown so big," which was an unwelcome twist on my name. Upon hearing that, my sister thought it was hilarious and started calling me "Kyon." Some friends who came to my house happened to overhear her calling me that, and ever since, my nickname's been Kyon. *Damn.*

"It's an annual family tradition for us cousins to get together during Golden Week."

And with that indifferent response, I continued trudging up the hill. The feeling of sweat dripping from my hair was extremely unpleasant.

Taniguchi was cheerfully going on about stuff like some cute girl he met at work and how he'd been saving up money so he had plenty to spend for a date. This could be considered some of the most boring information ever told, along with telling people about your dreams, or bragging about your pet.

As I listened to Taniguchi describe three different date scenarios with his nonexistent companion, we finally made it to the school front gate.

When I entered the classroom, I found that Haruhi Suzumiya was already in the seat behind mine, coolly looking out the window. Today, her hair was arranged in two buns sticking out like doorknobs, which made me think, *Ah, two spots would make today Wednesday,* and with that affirmation, I took my seat. That was when I probably became possessed by some demon. I can think of no other explanation. The next thing I knew, I was talking to Haruhi Suzumiya.

"Do you change your hair every day for the aliens?"

Haruhi turned her head towards me in a robotic motion and stared at me with her perpetually serious face. Kinda scary.

"When did you notice?" she asked in a tone like she was talking to a rock on the side of the road.

Come to think of it, when did I notice?

"Hmm . . . just recently."

"I see."

Haruhi rested her chin on her hand, looking like she was already sick of this.

"I think that each day of the week gives off a different image."

This would be the first time we actually reached a conversation.

"Just look at the Chinese characters used for the names of the days of the week. Color-wise, Monday (Moon) would be yellow. Tuesday (Fire) is red. Wednesday (Water) is blue. Thursday (Wood) is green. Friday (Gold) would be gold. Saturday (Earth) would be light brown. Sunday (Sun) would be white."

I guess I can see where she's coming from.

"So with numbers, Monday would be zero and Sunday would be six?"

"Yes."

"Monday feels more like one to me."

"Nobody asked for your opinion."

"Oh, really?"

Haruhi continued to stare as though she found something wrong with my muttering face. This lasted long enough for me to start feeling quite uneasy.

She asked, "Have I met you before? A long time ago?"

"Nope," I replied. And with homeroom teacher Okabe's entrance, the conversation came to an end.

That was the beginning. Nothing particularly significant, but it was indeed the catalyst.

Besides, Haruhi was only in the classroom during class so the only time I could talk to her was right before homeroom. And I can't deny the fact that being seated right in front of her provided the perfect position for casually striking up a conversation with her.

In any case, a serious response from Haruhi was a surprise. "Shut up!" "Moron!" "Be quiet!" "Who cares about that?!" were the replies I was expecting. The fact that I still talked to her anyway probably means there's something wrong with me.

Which is why when Haruhi showed up the next day without her hair tied off in three spots according to pattern, but with her long, beautiful black hair cut instead, I was rather disturbed. Anyway, wasn't cutting it the day after I pointed it out a bit hasty? What gives?

Upon asking, Haruhi replied, "None of your business."

As usual, she merely sounded pissed without actually revealing what she was thinking. There was no way she was going to tell me why she cut her hair.

Well, I expected as much.

"Did you really try joining all the clubs?"

Afterward, conversing with Haruhi in the short period before homeroom became a daily event. Not only did I have to initiate the conversation every time, I had to be careful in choosing subject matter since talking about what was on TV yesterday or the weather would elicit a "that's dead boring" reaction from Haruhi.

"Let me know if you find one that's fun. It'd be useful to know."

"There aren't any."

An immediate response.

"There totally aren't any at all."

After repeating herself, Haruhi exhaled like butterfly wings fluttering. Was that supposed to be a sigh?

"I was expecting something better after entering high school, but this is no different than back in grammar and middle school. Maybe I chose the wrong place."

"What criteria did *you* use to choose a school?"

"The athletic and arts clubs are all so normal. With so many clubs, you'd think there'd be at least one weird one."

"How exactly do you decide if it's normal or weird?"

"Any club I like is weird. Everything else is totally normal. Isn't that obvious?"

"Really? Obvious, is it? First I've heard about it."

"Hmph."

She looked away, and the day's conversation came to an end.

Another day came.

"I heard this rumor."

"Probably something worthless, right?"

"Is it true that you've dumped every guy you went out with?"

"What gives you the right to ask me that?"

Haruhi brushed her hair off her shoulder and glared at me with her dark black eyes. Man, the only time her face showed any emotion was when she was pissed off.

"You heard that from Taniguchi? I can't believe I'm still in the same class with him in high school. Maybe he's a stalker."

"I doubt it." I think.

"I don't know what you've heard, but fine. It's probably all true."

"There seriously wasn't a single guy you wanted to go out with?"

"Totally not."

It appeared she had a habit of using the word "totally."

"Every single one of them was ridiculously lame. Meet in front of the station on Sunday and do something obvious like watch a movie, go to the amusement park, or watch a sporting event. Then have lunch at a fast food place. Wander around and get a drink. Bye, see you tomorrow. What, that's it?"

I was wondering what she found wrong with that, but I kept my mouth shut. If Haruhi thinks there's a problem, then by all means, a problem there must be.

"And what's up with most of them asking me out over the phone? Important matters like that should be done in person!"

As I channeled the psyche of a guy who probably found it hard to make such an important — at least for him — confession while being glared at like an insect, I decided to play along for now.

"Well, I guess so. I'd probably just ask her in person."

"That's not important!"

Make up your mind.

"The problem is that every man on this planet is worthless. Honestly, I was irritated for most of middle school."

You still are.

"Then what kind of a guy did you want? I'm guessing an alien?"

"An alien. Or something along those lines. In any case, as long as they aren't an ordinary human, it doesn't matter if they're male or female."

"Why are you so particular about non-humans?" As soon as I asked, Haruhi looked at me like I was retarded.

"Isn't that more fun?!"

I suppose . . . she might be right.

I won't argue with Haruhi's opinion. I wouldn't mind if a mysterious, beautiful transfer student was actually half-alien, half-human. And if that moron Taniguchi, sitting nearby trying to spy on Haruhi and me, had actually been an investigator from the future, that would have been pretty cool. And if Ryoko Asakura, who was smiling in my direction for some reason, had actually been an esper, life at school would have been a bit more fun.

But it's all impossible. Aliens, time travelers, and espers couldn't possibly exist. Even if they did, they wouldn't just pop up in front of us. Besides, there's no way someone would walk up to me and say, "Hey. Guess what? I'm actually an alien," by way of introduction for no reason at all.

"And that's why!" Haruhi yelled out, knocking her chair down in the process. Everyone in the class turned around.

"And that's why I'm working so hard!"

"Sorry I'm late!" Our homeroom teacher, Okabe, looking bright, cheerful and out of breath, rushed in, took a look at Haruhi, standing with her fist in the air and glaring at the ceiling, and at everybody else in the classroom looking at Haruhi in unison, and froze in bewilderment.

"Ah . . . homeroom's starting."

Haruhi plopped back into her chair and began fervently staring at a corner of her desk. Whew.

I turned back toward the front of the room, the rest of the class did the same, and teacher Okabe staggered over to his podium and cleared his throat.

"Sorry I'm late. Ah . . . homeroom's starting."

And with that reiteration of his opening remarks, we returned to our daily mundane routine. This daily mundane routine is probably what Haruhi detested most.

But isn't that how life goes?

Still. I couldn't ignore this crazy feeling in the dark corner of my heart that envied Haruhi's way of life.

She was still eagerly waiting for a chance encounter with the extraordinary, something I had given up on long ago. And you can't deny that she was going all out for it. It's not like aliens are going to fall out of the sky if you wait long enough. Haruhi's point was that in that case, we should reach out to them. Thus, the markings on the grounds, the painting on the roof, and the talismans around school.

Geez Louise. (Do people even say that anymore?)

I don't know when Haruhi began doing things to make spectators think she's some sort of mental patient. But I guess that if she had already spent a long time waiting before running out of patience, and attempting bizarre rituals with no results, it would make perfect sense for her to end up always looking like she hated the whole world, right? Or I guess not.

"Hey, Kyon."

During break, Taniguchi came over with a moody expression plastered on his face. "That expression really makes you look like a moron, Taniguchi."

"Screw you. Forget about that. Anyway, what kind of magic did you use, Kyon?"

"What do you mean by magic?" I responded, as I recalled the saying that sufficiently advanced technology is indistinguishable from magic.

Sticking his thumb at Haruhi's seat, which Haruhi, true to form, had vacated the instant class ended, Taniguchi said, "I've never seen Suzumiya talk that long before. What did you say to her?"

"Dunno. What did I say? I get the feeling I just asked whatever was on my mind."

Taniguchi had this overly exaggerated look of shock on this face. "It's the end of the world." Kunikida popped out from behind him.

"Kyon's always liked weird girls."

"Don't say things that can be misconstrued," I replied.

"I don't give a damn about whether or not Kyon likes weird girls," said Taniguchi. "What I want to understand is how Suzumiya and Kyon managed to hold an actual conversation. I can't accept it."

"If I had to guess, wouldn't it be because Kyon would also be categorized as a weirdo?"

"Well, yeah. A guy with a nickname like Kyon can't be normal. But still."

Stop going "Kyon, Kyon." Hell, I'd rather have you call me by my actual name. I would at least like my little sister to call me "Big Brother."

"I'd also like to know."

A girl's voice suddenly descended upon us. A clear soprano. I looked up to find Ryoko Asakura with a sincere smile on her face.

"Suzumiya never responds no matter how hard I try. How did you get her to talk to you? Is there a trick to it?"

I gave it a little consideration. Or I should say, pretended to give it consideration before shaking my head. The answer was obvious, after all.

"I don't know."

Asakura laughed.

"Hmm. But I'm relieved now. I'd be worried if Suzumiya kept isolating herself from the rest of the class. It's a good thing that she's managed to make a friend."

If you're wondering why Ryoko Asakura was acting concerned as though she were class president, that's because she was the class president. It had been decided in the long homeroom period earlier.

"Friend, huh. . . ."

I tilted my head. You think so? I get the feeling I've only ever seen her with a sullen expression on her face.

"Keep up whatever you're doing to make Suzumiya open up to the class. We were fortunate enough to be put into the same class, so we should all be friends, right? I'm counting on you."

Counting on me, huh? Easy for you to say.

"If I need to tell her anything from now on, I'll ask you to pass on the message for me."

Wait, hold on. I'm not her spokesperson or anything.

"Pretty please?"

She even clasped her hands together. I could only stammer grunts in the form of "ah" and "uh" which she apparently took to mean my consent. And with a smile like a yellow tulip in our direction, she returned to the cluster of girls. The fact that every girl in that cluster was turning their attention this way was enough to sink my mood another two notches.

"Kyon, we're buddies, right?"

Taniguchi said this with a suspicious glint in his eyes. What was he talking about? Even Kunikida was standing there with his eyes closed and arms crossed while nodding his head for no reason.

Guys are all idiots.

Apparently, it was decided at some point that the seating order was to be changed every month. Class president Ryoko Asakura went around with a cookie tin of quadruple-folded pieces of paper to be drawn. I drew a quite excellent seat next to the window facing the courtyard, second from the back of the room. And as for the person in the seat behind me, I don't know how it happened, but Haruhi Suzumiya sat behind me looking like she was suffering a cavity.

"I wonder if students will start disappearing one by one. Or maybe a teacher will be found murdered inside a locked classroom."

"That's some dangerous stuff."

"There was a Mystery Research Society."

"Heh. How was it?"

"A joke. They haven't encountered anything remotely resembling a case. All the members are just mystery novel fanatics. None of them look like detective material."

"Well, duh."

"I was expecting more from the Supernatural Phenomena Research Society."

"Really."

"But it was just a bunch of occult freaks. What do you think of that?"

"Not much."

"Oh, man. It's boring! Why doesn't this school have a single decent club?"

"You can't do anything about what doesn't exist."

"I expected high school to have more radical clubs. I feel like a stupid baseball player aiming for the national championships who just discovered that this high school doesn't even have a baseball team."

Haruhi glared at the sky with crocodile eyes like those of an enchantress ready to begin a one-hundred-prayer ritual and sighed like a breeze.

Was I supposed to feel sorry for her?

All else aside, Haruhi hadn't even specified what kind of a club would satisfy her. Did she even know? She was just vaguely thinking, "I want to do something fun." What would the "something fun" be? Solving a homicide? Looking for aliens? Exorcising demons? I got the feeling she hadn't even decided yet.

I offered my opinion: "In the end, humans have to settle for what's in front of them. If you think about it, the only humans who couldn't were the ones who made discoveries or inventions and advanced civilization. Planes were invented because people wanted to fly. Cars and trains came to be because people wanted easier means to move around. But this all came from a limited number of people who had innovative plans and concepts. In other words, geniuses made it all possible. Average people like us are best off living ordinary lives."

"Shut up."

Haruhi cut me off and turned away, just as I was getting into a groove. She looked like she was in a really bad mood. Well, nothing new about that.

That girl probably didn't care what it was as long as it was a phenomenon that defied the tedium of reality. But such a phenomenon wasn't going to readily appear in this world. Or rather, it wasn't going to appear, period.

Long live the laws of physics! They're what allow us to live life in peace and quiet. Too bad for Haruhi.

At least that's what I thought.

That's normal, right?

What was the catalyst here?

Maybe our last conversation gave her the idea.

It happened so fast.

Bright rays of sunlight were putting me to sleep as my head perilously swayed back and forth, to and fro. I felt something grab my collar and pull with frightful vigor. Exhausted, I felt the back of my head meet the edge of the desk behind me with a fierce crash. I could feel fresh tears in my eyes.

"What are you doing?!"

When I turned around in rage and indignation, I found Haruhi standing and grabbing my collar with — for the first time ever — a smile reminiscent of a blazing sun in an equatorial sky. If you could take the temperature of a smile, hers would have matched the climate in the middle of a rain forest.

"I figured it out!"

Don't spit on me.

"Why didn't I realize such a simple thing sooner?!"

Haruhi looked at me with her eyes shining as brightly as Alpha Cygni. I had no choice but to ask.

"Realize what?"

"If there aren't any, I just have to make one myself!"

"Make what?"

"A club!"

It appears that being pressed up against the desk wasn't the only reason my head was hurting.

"I see. That's great. By the way, you can let go now."

"What's with your reaction? You should be a little happier about this discovery!"

"You can tell me all about your discovery later. Depending on the circumstances, I may even share your joy. But for now, just calm down."

"What do you mean?"

"We're in class right now."

Haruhi finally released her grip on my collar. As I turned my ringing head back toward the front of the room, I could see my fellow classmates with their mouths half-open and the female teacher, fresh out of college, with a piece of chalk in one hand, on the verge of tears.

I gestured behind me for Haruhi to hurry up and sit down. Then I turned my hand palm-up and held it out toward the poor English teacher.

Please continue with class.

As she muttered something under her breath, Haruhi finally took her seat, and the female teacher went back to writing on the board.

Make a new club?

Hmm.

She couldn't possibly be including me as a member, right?

The throbbing in the back of my head boded of ill things to come.

CHAPTER 2

In retrospect, that was exactly how it played out.

The following break, Haruhi didn't leave the room by herself like normal. Instead, she walked out with my arm forcibly in tow. After exiting the classroom, she rapidly proceeded through the hallway and flew up a flight of stairs before stopping in front of the door which led to the rooftop terrace.

The door to the roof was usually locked and the staircase leading up from the fourth floor was mostly used for storage, probably by the Art Club. Stuff like huge canvases, broken easels, and noseless busts of Mars were all piled up, leaving the corridor feeling cramped. Scratch that, it *was* cramped. And the lighting was dim to boot.

What was the point of bringing me to a place like this?

"Help me," Haruhi said. She was currently grabbing my necktie, pressuring me with her penetrating eyes. It felt like extortion.

"Help you with what?"

I already knew the answer, but I asked anyway.

"Making my new club."

"Why do I have to help with your idea? Tell me that first."

"I'll go secure a room and members and you go get the chartering paperwork."

She's not listening.

I untangled myself from Haruhi's grip.

"What kind of club are you planning on making?"

"Why does that even matter? Creating the club comes first!"

I highly doubted the school would accept a club engaging in undisclosed activities.

"Understand? Find out what you have to do before school's over. I'll find a room before then. Got it?"

No. Except I got the feeling that if I gave voice to that thought, I would be clubbed to death on the spot. While I was trying to say the right thing, Haruhi had already flitted down the stairs with an oddly spry skipping motion, leaving behind a very confused boy at the top of the dusty stairway.

". . . I didn't say yes or no yet. . . ."

No point in talking to a plaster bust. I set off, now thinking about what I would say to my curious classmates when I returned to the classroom.

Here are the provisions for chartering a "student association."

Five or more members. Determine faculty advisor, name, responsible party, and club activities. These must be approved by the student council club administration committee. Club activities must adhere to the policy of leading a productive and active school life. Based on future activities and performance, the administration committee may press a motion for a raise in status to "research society." Furthermore, as long as the group remains a student association, no funding will be provided.

There was no need for any real digging. This was all written in the back of the student handbook.

We could take care of the member requirement by randomly

asking people to let us use their names. A faculty advisor might be hard to find, but there was always the option of using deceit. The name just needed to be something inoffensive. The responsible party would obviously be Haruhi.

But I was willing to bet that her club activities weren't going to "adhere to the policy of leading a productive and active school life."

At least that's what I told her. However, Haruhi Suzumiya is the kind of person who only hears what she wants to hear.

Grabbing the sleeve of my blazer with a vise-like grip the moment the bell rang, Haruhi dragged me out of the room the way a kidnapper would and zoomed off. It was all I could do to prevent my bookbag from being left behind in the classroom.

"Where are we going?" The question any sane person would ask in this scenario.

"The club room!" was Haruhi's curt response before she fell silent as she moved forward with enough vigor to bowl over the darting students in front of us. At least let go of my arm!

We navigated through a passage and descended to the first floor before exiting. Then we entered a different building and headed back upstairs before Haruhi came to a stop in the middle of a dimly lit hallway, forcing me to brake as well.

A door stood before us.

Literary Club.

That's what it said on the affixed, slanting nameplate.

"Here."

Haruhi opened the door without even knocking and barged in without the slightest hint of reservation. I followed suit, naturally.

The room was surprisingly large. Maybe because it only contained a long table, metal chairs, and steel bookshelves. The two or three cracks running across the ceiling and walls told the tale of the decrepit state of the building structure.

And seated in one of the metal chairs, like an addition to the room, was a girl reading a thick hardcover book.

"This room is now our club room!" Haruhi proclaimed in a dignified fashion, throwing her arms into the air. Her face was painted with a divine smile. I decided not to voice my opinion that seeing such a smile on her face in the classroom every day would be a good thing.

"Wait a second. Where are we?"

"The cultural department clubhouse. The art club and wind ensemble have the art room and music room, right? Clubs and societies that don't have specialized classrooms have rooms in this clubhouse. Also known as the old shack. This is the literary club's room."

"So this belongs to the literary club."

"But the third-years all graduated last spring so it has zero members. It was the only club that would have been cut if nobody new joined. And this girl is the first-year who joined."

"Then the club wasn't cut, right?"

"It might as well have been. It only has one person."

Unfreakingbelievable. She planned on taking over the room. I directed my attention toward the girl who was apparently a first-year literary club member, indulging herself in reading at the folding table.

A girl with short hair and glasses.

She hadn't even looked up once during Haruhi's clamoring. The only movement was when her fingers turned the page every once in a while. The rest of her body hadn't moved the slightest bit. She was completely ignoring our presence. She was quite the weird girl.

I lowered my voice and whispered to Haruhi, "What about her?"

"She said she's fine with it."

"For real?"

"I ran into her during lunch. When I asked her to lend me this room, she said to go ahead. She doesn't care as long as she can read apparently. I suppose you could call her an oddball."

You're one to talk.

I took another look at the strange literary club member.

Pale skin with a face devoid of emotion. Robotic finger movement. Her hair was shorter than a bob cut yet managed to cover her arranged features. It made me want to see what she looked like without glasses on. Her doll-like demeanor meant she had a lack of presence. If I had to classify her, the simplest way would be to say she's the mysterious, stoic type.

I'm not sure what she thought of my blatantly fixed stare. The girl pushed up the bridge of her glasses without preamble.

Dark-colored eyes stared at me from behind the lenses. Neither eyes nor lips revealed any emotion at all. A top-notch poker face. Unlike Haruhi's, her default expression appeared to show no emotion at all.

"Yuki Nagato," she said. Seemed to be her name. She had a flat voice you could forget in three seconds.

Yuki Nagato looked at me for about as long as it would take to blink twice. She then apparently lost interest and returned to her reading.

"So, Nagato," I said. "She's planning on turning this room into an I-have-no-idea-what club. Is that still okay with you?"

"Yes."

Yuki Nagato answered without taking her eyes from the page.

"Well, but, it'll probably be a huge bother."

"Not really."

"You might even get chased out."

"Go ahead."

Quick responses were good, but her replies had no feeling to them. It would seem that she genuinely didn't care.

"Well. There you have it," Haruhi interjected. Her voice was always full of life. I was getting a bad feeling about this for some reason.

"Be sure to meet in this room after school from now on. You had better show up! If you don't, heads will roll."

She said this with a smile like cherry blossoms in full bloom. I reluctantly nodded my assent.

Since I like my head where it is.

And so we managed to secure a club room, which was good, but we hadn't yet made any progress with the paperwork. Besides, we hadn't even decided on a name or what club activities we'd be engaging in. I told her to figure those out first, but Haruhi apparently had other ideas.

"That stuff will all fall into place later on," Haruhi loudly proclaimed. "First comes the members. We need at least two more."

Which means what? You're counting that literary club member? Aren't you confusing Yuki Nagato with a piece of furniture that came with the room?

"Rest assured, I'll find them in no time. I happen to know of someone who was made for this club."

How was I supposed to rest assured? My doubts were only growing stronger.

The next day, I declined when Taniguchi and Kunikida invited me to walk home with them and, having no choice, dragged my legs toward the club room.

Haruhi just yelled, "You go on ahead!" before tearing out of the room with a record acceleration time that would explain why the track team so fervently pursued her membership. Fast enough to make you wonder if she might have rocket boosters attached to her legs. She was probably off to secure the new club member. Did she finally run into an alien?

I slung my bookbag over my shoulder and unenthusiastically shuffled my feet in the direction of the literary club.

Yuki Nagato was already in the club room. She was reading in the exact same position as yesterday, giving me this sense of déjà vu. And just like yesterday, she didn't even twitch as I entered the room. Not that I would know, but is the literary club just a club for sitting around and reading books?

Silence.

". . . What'cha reading?" I asked, unable to bear the silence any longer. Instead of answering, Yuki Nagato merely raised the book to show me the cover. The foreign-sounding title, written in gothic lettering, was already putting me to sleep. Looked like a sci-fi novel or something.

"Is it any good?"

Yuki Nagato pushed up the bridge of her glasses with a limp motion and replied in a listless tone.

"Unique."

I got the feeling she was just giving an arbitrary answer to my question.

"Which part of it?"

"All of it."

"You like books, huh?"

"Relatively."

"Is that so. . . ."

". . ."

Silence.

Can I leave now?

I dropped my bag on the table and was in the process of seating myself in one of the extra chairs when the door opened. More like it was kicked open.

"Hey! Sorry about being late! It took a while to catch her!"

Haruhi made her entrance with one hand held over her head. Her other hand was behind her, grabbing some other person's arm. Haruhi barged in with said person in tow, obviously brought here against their will, and locked the door for some reason.

Click. Upon hearing that sound, the petite person began trembling with anxiety. It was another girl.

And an extraordinarily beautiful one at that.

How is this person "made for this club," exactly?

"What is this?" the beautiful girl said. The poor thing was almost in tears.

"Where are we? Why did you bring me here? Why are you l-locking the door?! What are you . . ."

"Be quiet."

The girl froze with a start upon hearing Haruhi's imperious voice.

"Allow me to introduce you. This is Mikuru Asahina."

And with that, Haruhi said no more. That's the whole introduction?

A constrained silence fell over the room. Haruhi was standing there looking like she'd already done her duty. Yuki Nagato was reading as though nothing had happened. The mysterious girl named Mikuru Asahina was cowering on the verge of tears. I didn't foresee any of them speaking up soon so I had no choice but to open my mouth.

"Where did you abduct her from?"

"I didn't abduct her. It was voluntary arrest."

Close enough.

"I caught her daydreaming in a second-year classroom. I walk through every nook and cranny of this school during breaks so her face started to become familiar after a while."

I had been wondering why she wasn't in the classroom during breaks. So that's what she was doing. Wait, more importantly . . .

"Then isn't she an upperclassman?"

"What about it?"

She had a puzzled expression on her face. Apparently, she really didn't think anything of it.

"Never mind, then . . . Uh, Asahina, is it? Why her?"

"Well, take a look."

Haruhi jabbed her finger at the nose of Mikuru Asahina, who shrank in fear.

"She's super cute, isn't she?"

Haruhi sounded like a dangerous kidnapper. At least that was my reaction.

"I believe that *moe* is an essential factor."

". . . Sorry. What was that?"

"*Moe*, you know, turn-ons. The element of turning people on. Fundamentally, in every story where something strange happens, there's always an alluring, Lolita-looking character present!"

I inadvertently turned to look at Mikuru Asahina. A petite body and a baby face. *I see.* An inattentive person could easily mistake her for a grade school student. Her slightly curly chestnut hair softly concealed her collar. Her watery puppy dog eyes begged for protection, and her teeth of white ivory peeking out from within her half-open mouth created a miraculous sense of harmony with her small face. If she had been holding a wand with a glowing ball on top, I'd have expected her to transform into a magical anime girl. Wait, what the hell am I saying?

"That's not all!"

Haruhi circled behind Mikuru Asahina, our upperclassman, with a lofty smile, and suddenly grabbed her from behind.

"Wahyaa —!" Asahina screamed. Haruhi, undeterred, moved in for the kill as she grabbed hold of her breasts through her sailor uniform.

"Ahh —!"

"She's so small, yet look. Her breasts are bigger than mine. A Lolita face with big breasts. This is an important element of turning people on!"

News to me.

"Ah — they sure are big. . . ." With that said, Haruhi reached under Asahina's uniform and began to grope her.

Hel-lo?

"It's starting to piss me off. Such a cutie's sporting bigger ones than me!"

Asahina struggled and kicked, her face bright red, but she couldn't overcome the difference between their physical builds. Haruhi, getting carried away, began lifting her skirt, which was when I pried the perverted girl off of Asahina's back.

"Are you a moron?"

"But they're really big! Seriously. Why don't you touch them?"

Asahina let out a small squeak upon hearing that.

"I'll pass."

What else could I say?

What's really amazing is that during this whole time, Yuki Nagato hadn't looked up from her book once. Something was wrong with her too.

"So then, what? The fact that this . . . Asahina is cute, small, and has big breasts is why you brought her here?"

"That's right."

Haruhi must have been born dumb.

"I was thinking that we need a mascot character like her."

Don't. Think about something else.

Asahina softly rearranged her disheveled uniform, then stared at me with upturned eyes.

It's kind of awkward when you look at me that way.

"Mikuru, are you in any other clubs?"

"Um . . . the calligraphy club . . ."

"Quit that then. It'll conflict with our club activities."

Haruhi was as self-centered as ever.

Asahina looked like a future murder victim who had just been given the option of taking potassium cyanide or strychnine. She glanced up at me once more as if seeking salvation. Then she noticed Yuki Nagato's presence for the first time, and her eyes opened wide in surprise. Her eyes wandered the room before she whispered, "I see. . . ." in a voice reminiscent of a dragonfly sighing.

"I understand," she said.

What did she just understand?

"I'll quit the calligraphy club and join this one."

The sadness in her voice really made me feel bad for her.

"But I'm not sure what the literary club does. . . ."

"We aren't the literary club."

Haruhi said this like it was the most obvious thing in the world. I explained to the wide-eyed Asahina in Haruhi's place.

"We're temporarily borrowing this room. The club you're being forced into is an unnamed student association, yet to be made by Suzumiya over there, that will participate in unknown activities."

"Wha . . . ?"

"Incidentally, the person sitting there reading is the real literary club member."

"Ah . . ."

Asahina, adorable lips wide open, became speechless. Couldn't blame her.

"No worries!"

Haruhi, with a bright smile free from any sense of responsibility, firmly brought her hand down onto Asahina's small shoulder.

"I just came up with a name!"

". . . Let's hear it."

My voice, carrying no hint of expectation, echoed through the room. If possible, I'd rather not hear this. And Haruhi Suzumiya obviously couldn't care less about my concerns as she triumphantly named the club in her soaring voice.

"Attention everyone. The name of this fledging club has just been decided. No alterations have been made. This is purely a product of Haruhi Suzumiya's mind.

"SOS Brigade.

"The Save the World by Overloading it with Fun Haruhi Suzumiya Brigade.

"Or SOS Brigade for short."

Feel free to laugh.

I was struck dumb first, though.

You're probably wondering why it's a brigade. Originally, it should have been the Save the World by Overloading it with Fun Haruhi Suzumiya Association, but an association hadn't even been chartered yet, and nobody had a clue as to what this group was supposed to do. "So brigade is fine then." Haruhi's incomprehensible words settled the matter. Oh, joy.

Asahina kept her mouth shut as though resigned to her fate. Yuki Nagato was an outsider. I couldn't bring myself to say anything. Consequently, the name "SOS Brigade" passed with one aye and three abstentions. Oh, joy.

Just do whatever you want.

After Haruhi instructed us to meet here after school every day, we were dismissed. The sight of Asahina trudging through the hallway with her shoulders drooped was just too pitiful to watch, so . . .

"Asahina."

"What is it?"

Asahina, who didn't look in any way older than me, tilted her innocent face, pure in essence, toward me.

"You don't have to join such a weird group. Don't worry about her. I'll talk to her later."

"No."

She stopped walking, and her eyes narrowed ever so slightly.

"It's OK. I'll join."

"But I really doubt this will turn out well."

"It'll be fine. You're also here, aren't you?"

That's right. Why am I here?

"This was probably an inevitability on this time plane. . . ."

The eyes on her cute, round face looked off into the distance.

"Huh?"

"And I'm concerned about why Nagato is here. . . ."

"Concerned?"

"Ah. No, it's nothing."

Asahina shook her head in a flustered state. The soft strands of her hair gently swayed.

Then Asahina, with an embarrassed smile on her face, bowed deeply.

"I may be new at this, but I hope to get along with everyone."

"Well, if you say so. . . ."

"Also, please feel free to call me Mikuru."

She smiled sweetly.

Yeah. She's cute enough to make me swoon.

I was talking to Haruhi one day.

"What else do you think we need?"

"Beats me."

"I'm thinking about getting my hands on a mysterious transfer student."

"I'd like you to define mysterious first."

"It hasn't even been two months since the new term began. Anyone who transfers in at this point must qualify as mysterious, right? Don't you agree?"

"Maybe the student's dad was suddenly transferred."

"No, that's abnormal."

"What would you consider normal? I'd like to know that."

"I wonder if a mysterious transfer student will show up."

"In other words, you don't give a damn what I think, do you?"

It would appear that a rumor had spread that Haruhi and I were plotting something.

"Say, what are you and Suzumiya up to?"

The person who asked this was obviously Taniguchi.

"Don't tell me you two are dating."

"Absolutely not." I'm the one who would like to know exactly what the hell we're doing.

"Don't overdo it. We're not in middle school anymore. If you render the grounds unusable, they might suspend you."

If Haruhi does something by herself, I can't be bothered to clean up after her. At the very least, I have to prevent Yuki Nagato and Mikuru Asahina from coming to any harm. I'm kind of proud of how considerate I am.

Though I doubt I have much chance of stopping Haruhi once the afterburners kick in.

After the SOS Brigade was founded, the literary club room, previously only adorned by a long table, metal chairs, and bookshelves, began accumulating a growing number of items.

I don't know where Haruhi got this stuff from, but a portable garment rack sat in the corner of the room along with an electric kettle, teapot, and enough teacups for everyone. The room also had a stereo system without a CD player, a single-compartment fridge in this day and age, a portable gas stove, an earthenware pot, and various eating utensils. What was all of this stuff for? Was she planning on living here?

Haruhi was currently sitting Indian style with her arms crossed on a desk she had filched from some classroom. And on the desk rested a pyramid on which the words *Brigade Chief* were written in magic marker.

"A computer would be nice, too," she said. "We're living in the information age and yet we don't have a single computer. I can't forgive them."

Can't forgive whom?

Our members were basically assembled. Yuki Nagato was in her usual position, engrossed in reading some hardcover with a title about some Saturn moon falling. Asahina, who really didn't need to come but obediently came anyway, was seated in a chair with nothing to do.

Haruhi leaped off the desk and smiled in my direction, giving me a really ominous feeling.

"So let's go scrounge one up." Haruhi said this looking like a deer hunter off to the hunting range.

"Scrounge up a computer? From where? Are you planning on raiding an electronics store?"

"Of course not. There's a much closer source."

After ordering us to follow her, Haruhi led Asahina and me to our destination, the Computer Research Society two doors down.

I see.

"Hold this," she said as she handed me an instant camera. "I'm going to tell you the plan, so you had better stick to it. Don't mess up the timing. Understood?"

Haruhi pulled me down and whispered her "plan" into my ear.

"Huh? That's ridiculous."

"It'll be fine."

Fine for you, maybe. I glanced at Asahina, who was curiously looking this way, and attempted to make eye contact.

It would be a good idea to run for it now.

As I furiously blinked my eyes at her, Asahina looked up at me dubiously, and after applying some kind of twisted logic, she blushed. No good. She wasn't getting the message.

In the meantime, Haruhi had calmly opened the door to the Computer Research Society without even knocking.

"Hello! We're here to take one set of computer and peripherals!"

The layout was similar to ours, but this club room was rather cramped. A number of display monitors and computer towers were on the uniformly spaced tables. The low whirring of cooling fans resonated through the room.

The four male students who had been clattering away on their keyboards turned their attention to Haruhi, standing in their doorway on some kind of mission.

"Who's in charge?" Haruhi said rather haughtily with a smile on her face. One of them stood in response.

"That would be me. Do you need something?"

"I already told you what I need. I only need one, so just give me a computer."

The Computer Research Society president, an unnamed upper-classman, had an expression on his face that plainly asked "What is she talking about?" as he shook his head.

"No way. School funding wasn't enough to cover the cost, so we had to save up our own money before we were able to finally buy these just recently. We aren't blessed with enough equipment to just hand some out to whoever asks for them."

"One can't hurt. You've got so many."

"Now look here . . . Wait. Who are you people?"

"The SOS brigade chief, Haruhi Suzumiya. These two are sub-ordinates number one and number two."

You didn't have to call us subordinates.

"I order it in the name of the SOS Brigade. Stop your grumbling and hand one over."

"I don't know who you people are, but no means no. Buy one yourself."

"In that case, I have my own ideas about that."

Haruhi's eyes shone with audacity. Not a good sign.

Pushing Asahina, who had been spacing out nearby, in front of her, Haruhi approached the president. And just when we realized that she'd grabbed the president's arm, she pressed his palm onto Asahina's breast with lightning speed.

"Ahh!"

"Noo!"

Click.

With two varying screams playing in the background, I clicked the shutter on the instant camera.

As she held down Asahina, who was trying to escape, Haruhi

used her right hand to direct the president's hand in firmly groping the little girl's breast.

"Kyon. Take another shot."

I reluctantly pressed the shutter button. Forgive me, Asahina
and unnamed president. The president finally broke free of
Haruhi's grip and leapt away right when Haruhi was about to
thrust his hand into Asahina's skirt.

"What are you doing?!"

Haruhi gracefully waved her finger in front of the president's
bright red face.

"Tsk. Tsk. Tsk. I've got pictures of your sexual harassment now.
If you don't want me to spread these pictures around school,
hand over a computer."

"That's ridiculous!" the president furiously objected. I feel
for you.

"You forced me to do it! I'm innocent!"

"And how many people do you think will believe you?"

I looked towards Asahina to find her unmoving, sprawled on
the floor. She'd moved beyond shock and into a coma.

Meanwhile, the president continued to protest.

"All the members here are witnesses! It was against my will!"

The three computer members who had been petrified with their
jaws hanging open apparently regained their senses and nodded.

"That's right."

"It wasn't the prez's fault."

However, such weak reciting in unison wasn't going to work on
Haruhi.

"I'll say that the whole club gang-raped her!"

Everyone in the room, including Asahina and myself, turned
pale. That's going too far.

"Su-Su-Su-Suzumiya . . . !"

Haruhi lightly kicked away Asahina's arms, which were cling-
ing to her leg, and haughtily puffed up her chest.

"What will it be? Are you going to hand it over or not?!"

The president's face, which had already gone from red to white, now became ashen.

He was finally defeated.

"Take whichever one you want. . . ."

The president collapsed into his chair. The other members ran over.

"Prez!"

"Hang in there!"

"Get a hold of yourself!"

His head was hung like a marionette whose strings had been cut. I may have been an accomplice in this travesty, but I couldn't help but feel sorry for him.

"Which one's the newest model?"

She was as cool-headed as ever.

"Why do I have to tell you that?!"

Haruhi responded by pointing to the camera in my hand.

"Damn it! That one."

Haruhi took a look at the tower computer's brand and model number and took out a slip of paper from her skirt pocket.

"I stopped by the computer shop yesterday and had an employee show me all the newest models. This wasn't one of them."

Her attention to detail was scaring me.

Haruhi circled the table checking every computer before pointing to one of them.

"Give me this one."

"Hold on! We just bought that last month. . . ."

"Camera, camera."

". . . Take it! You thief!"

We are indeed thieves. I cannot deny it.

There was no end to Haruhi's demands. After disconnecting all the cables, she ordered that the monitor and every little thing be moved to the literary club and reconnected. She even had them run a LAN cable between our rooms so we could access the

Internet and connect through the school's domain on top of that. All of this was done by the Computer Society members. This is what you call extortion.

"Asahina."

Having been rendered helpless during this whole incident, I turned to the petite girl curled up in a fetal position with her hands over her face.

"Let's go back for now."

"Uhhh . . ."

I helped the sobbing Asahina up. Haruhi could have just let her own breasts be groped. If she doesn't give a damn about changing in front of guys, she probably wouldn't have a problem with that. As I tried to comfort Asahina, still crying, I wondered what the computer was going to be used for.

Well, I would find out soon enough.

The launch of the SOS Brigade Web site.

Apparently, that's what Haruhi wanted to do. "So? Who's going to make it? The Web site or whatever."

"You."

That was Haruhi's response.

"You've got free time, don't you? Do it. I have to find more members."

The computer was on the desk with the "Brigade Chief" pyramid. Haruhi was moving the mouse around and surfing the Web.

"Have it finished in a day or two. We can't participate in any activities until a site's up."

Yuki Nagato, reading her book, and Mikuru Asahina, sprawled on the table next to her, shoulders trembling, acted like they had nothing to do with this. It would appear that the only one listening to Haruhi talking was me. And since I was the only one who heard Haruhi's order, I had to follow through on it. At least, that's what Haruhi thought, no doubt about it.

"Easy for you to say."

At least, that's what I said, but I was actually pretty psyched. No. It's not that I'd gotten used to following Haruhi's orders. I was psyched about making the Web site. I'd never made one before, but it sounds pretty fun, right?

And that was that. The next day would be the first chapter of my epic struggle to make a Web site.

That being said, it wasn't much of a struggle at all. The Computer Research Society, living up to its name, had already installed most of the necessary programs. All I had to do was open up a template and do a bit of copy-and-pasting.

The problem was what to put on the site.

After all, I still had no idea what kind of activities the SOS Brigade was involved in. I couldn't possibly write about club activities that didn't exist yet, so after pasting an image saying *Welcome to the SOS Brigade's Website!* on the top page, my fingers stopped moving. I could hear the chants of "Hurry up and make it!" incessantly ringing through my ears, which is why I was sitting there with mouse in hand as I ate my lunch.

"Nagato, do you have anything you want to put on the site?"

I tried asking Yuki Nagato, who sat reading in our room even during lunch time.

"Nothing."

She didn't even look up. Not that I care, but she does go to class, right?

I returned my attention from Yuki Nagato to the 17-inch monitor and went back to thinking.

There's another problem. Isn't it a bad idea to use a school domain address for the Web site of a questionable brigade that holds lower status than a school-approved student association?

"What they don't know can't hurt 'em." That was Haruhi's defense. "If they find out about it, just drop the site. With these things, whoever takes action wins!"

I was a bit envious of her optimistic attitude.

I added a free CGI access counter, put up a text message address — still too early for a message board — and uploaded the Web site consisting of a top page alone with no actual content.

This should be good enough.

After confirming that the page was loading properly on the Net, I closed all the programs and shut down the computer. Then, as I was about to stretch myself out, I noticed Yuki Nagato standing behind me and jumped out of the chair.

It's like you couldn't sense her presence. Before I knew it, Yuki Nagato was standing behind me with a pale face that resembled a Noh mask. With a poker face you'd find yourself hard-pressed to match, she stared at me the way one would stare at an eye chart.

"Here."

She held out a thick book. Out of reflex, I took it. It sure was heavy. Looking at the cover, I saw that it was the sci-fi book Nagato had been reading a few days ago.

"I'll lend you this."

With that brief statement, Nagato left the room before I even had time to refuse. What's the point in lending me such a thick book? Left alone in the classroom, I could hear the bell signaling the approaching end of lunch break. It appeared that I was surrounded by people who couldn't care less about what I thought.

Upon returning to the classroom with the hardcover book, I was greeted by the point of a mechanical pencil poking me in the back.

"Well? Is the site done?"

Haruhi was sprawled on her desk with a sullen look on her face. She was furiously writing away about who knows what on a torn-out sheet of notebook paper. I feigned casualness to avoid the attention of fellow classmates.

"It's done, sure. But it's an empty site that'll probably piss off visitors."

"That's good enough for now. We just need an e-mail address."

"Wouldn't a text message address work, then?"

"That won't do. It wouldn't be able to handle the flood of e-mails."

"Why would a newly created e-mail address get flooded with e-mails?"

"That's a secret."

Then she got that disturbing smile on her face again. It gave me the creeps.

"You'll find out after school. For now, it's top secret."

I'd rather you keep it top secret forever.

Haruhi was nowhere to be seen during the following period. One could hope that she'd quietly gone home, but that was frankly impossible. Merely a prelude to her evildoings.

After school, I still had my misgivings about what we were doing — so why is it that my legs were taking me toward the club room? As I was making such metaphysical observations, I found myself in front of the door.

" 'Sup!"

Yuki Nagato was already there, naturally, along with Mikuru Asahina, sitting in a chair with her hands together.

I'm not one to talk, but are these two really that bored?

Asahina greeted me with what was obviously an expression of relief upon my entrance. I guess being stuck in a room alone with Nagato was stressful.

"You still came today after what happened yesterday?"

"Where's Suzumiya?" asked Asahina.

"Beats me. She was already gone during sixth period. Perhaps she's off extorting more equipment."

"Will I be forced to do something like yesterday again?"

Seeing that her brow was creased with worry, I tried to sound as kind as possible.

"Don't worry. The next time she tries to force you into something like that, I'll do everything I can to prevent it. She can use her own body for that stuff. It'd be a cinch for Suzumiya to pull off."

"Thank you."

The sight of her bowing her head with a shy smile on her face was so adorable that I wanted to throw my arms around her. I didn't, though.

"I'm counting on you, then."

"You can count on me."

My guarantee might have meant something if it hadn't fallen apart like a baseless theory, a house of cards, or an atom of hydrogen inside the sun, before even five minutes had passed. I'm worthless.

"Hey, hey!" Haruhi said as she entered the room. My eyes were drawn to the large paper bags in both of her hands.

"Took a little longer than expected. Sorry about that."

It's safe to assume that whenever Haruhi is in a good mood, she's plotting some scheme that involves inconveniencing other people.

Haruhi set the paper bags on the floor and turned to lock the door. Asahina reflexively jumped at the sound.

"What are you planning on doing this time, Suzumiya? Just so you know, I refuse to do any more burglary. Or blackmail," I said.

"What are you talking about? I'd never do anything like that."

"Then explain the computer on the desk."

"Obtained using peaceful measures. Forget that. Here. Look at this."

Haruhi removed a stack of printer paper from one of the paper bags. There was some kind of writing printed on the paper.

"These are flyers I made to spread the name of the SOS Brigade. I snuck into the copy room and printed out 200 copies."

Haruhi passed out the flyers to us. So that's what she was doing when she skipped class, huh? Pretty amazing how nobody caught her. I didn't particularly want to look at the flyer, but for the time being, I took it and gave it a glance.

PROCLAMATION OF THE SOS BRIGADE'S FOUNDING PRINCIPLES

We members of the SOS Brigade are searching for the mysteries of the world. People who have experienced something mysterious in the past, people who have run into something mysterious recently, and people who plan on a mysterious experience in the near future should come see us! We will solve your problem on the spot! Guaranteed. However, a normal mystery will not do. It has to be a mystery that wows us. Make note of that! You can contact us at . . .

I thought I was starting to understand the purpose of this brigade. It would appear that Haruhi wanted to immerse herself in the worlds of sci-fi, fantasy, and horror.

"Let's go pass them out now."

"Where at?"

"The front gate. There should be plenty of students heading home right now."

"Oh, really," was my response as I moved to pick up the paper bag, before Haruhi stopped me.

"You don't need to come. Mikuru's the one who's coming with me."

"What?"

Asahina, holding the half-sheet of paper in her hands and reading its poorly written contents, tilted her head. Haruhi rummaged through the other paper bag and vigorously pulled an item out.

"Ta-da!"

Looking as triumphant as an Olympic gold medalist, Haruhi pulled out what first appeared to be a piece of black cloth. But oh no —! Once Haruhi had finished removing objects from her bottomless bag, I realized why Haruhi had designated Asahina for the task and began praying for her. May your soul rest in peace.

Black leotard, fishnet stockings, attachable ears, and a bow tie along with a white collar, cuffs, and tail.

It looked undeniably like a bunny girl outfit.

"Um, um, um, what is this for?"

That was Asahina, sounding quite frightened.

"Can't you tell? *Bunny girl.*"

That was Haruhi, sounding quite calm.

"Y-Y-You can't mean for me to wear . . ."

"Of course. There's one for me, too."

"I-I can't wear something like that!"

"Don't worry. The size should be right."

"That's not what I meant. Um, are we going to wear those while passing out flyers at the school gate. . . ."

"Isn't that obvious?"

"I-I don't want to!"

"Shut up."

Crap. She had that flinty look in her eyes. Haruhi leapt onto Asahina the way a lioness would attack a stray gazelle and began removing the sailor uniform from the struggling girl.

"Noooo!"

"Stop resisting!"

Making outrageous demands, Haruhi pinned down Asahina. She easily pulled off her top and moved her fingers to the hook of the skirt, which is when I thought I better stop this and moved toward them only to meet Asahina's eyes.

"Don't look!"

Upon hearing that cry, I did an about-face and ran to the door — damn, it was locked — and wasted time rattling and turning the knob before I finally unlocked the door and tumbled outside.

And based on a quick side glance during all of this, Yuki Nagato was reading her book as though nothing was happening.

Don't you have anything to say about this?

As I leaned against the closed door, I could hear . . .

"Ah!" "No!" "At least . . . l-let me undress myself . . . Noo!"

. . . pitiable screams from Asahina . . .

"Ergh! C'mon! Take it all off! You should have listened to me to begin with!"

. . . and such triumphant battle cries from Haruhi.

Meh. I'd be lying if I said I didn't want to know what was going on in there, naturally.

Some time later, I received a signal.

"You can come in now!"

When I hesitantly returned to the room, I was met by the sight of two unbelievably perfect bunny girls. Haruhi and Asahina both looked amazing.

Low cut in front with an open back. High cut on the bottom with fishnet stockings wrapped around the legs. The bunny ears swaying on top of their heads and white collar and cuffs scored bonus points. Not that I knew what the points were for.

The combination of Haruhi, who has a slender build yet with curves, and Asahina, who looks small yet sticks out in all the right places, was too much for my eyes.

As I pondered if I should say "It looks good on you" to the sobbing Asahina, Haruhi spoke.

"What do you think?"

What do I think? I can only think that your mental capabilities are suspect.

"This'll be perfect for attracting attention! Most of the people walking by will take our flyers if we're dressed like this. Right?"

"Well, yeah. Two people dressed in costumes standing around school are bound to attract attention. . . . What about Nagato?"

"I could only buy two of them. I got the full set so it was expensive."

"Where do they sell this stuff?"

"I ordered it online."

". . . I see."

I was wondering why I didn't have to look down as much as usual when I noticed she was even careful enough to put on high heels.

Haruhi grabbed the bag containing the flyers.

"Let's go, Mikuru!"

Asahina, with her arms crossed over her chest, looked toward me for salvation. I could only stare at her in her bunny outfit.

Sorry. To be honest, I can't get enough of that outfit.

Asahina fussed like a child as she clung to the table, but being no match for Haruhi's ridiculous strength, she and her soft cries were swiftly dragged off, and the two bunny girls disappeared from the room. I sank into my chair with an overwhelming feeling of guilt.

"There."

Yuki Nagato pointed at the floor. Upon looking, I found two sailor uniforms lying in a scattered heap and . . . was that a bra?

The short-haired, bespectacled girl remained silent as her finger shifted to the garment rack before she wordlessly went back to reading as though her job was finished.

You do it, her gesture said.

Sighing, I picked up the girls' uniforms and hung them on the garment rack. Gah. I could still feel the warmth from their body heat.

Thirty minutes later, a worn-out Asahina returned. Whoa. Her eyes were red like a real bunny's. This isn't the time to be saying that. I quickly stood and gave her my chair. And just like before, Asahina collapsed onto the table, her finely-shaped shoulder blades trembling. Apparently, she didn't even have the energy to get changed. Her back was half exposed, making it difficult for my eyes. I removed my blazer and covered her quivering, pale back. The uncontrollably sobbing girl, the unresponsive book-worm, and the bewildered, castrated bastard (me) spent the following period of time silently in the club room with a record-setting strained atmosphere. In the distance, I could clearly hear the lousy horns of the brass band and indiscernible yelling of the baseball team.

It was around when I started thinking about such insignificant things as what dinner would be tonight that Haruhi made her heroic return. The first thing out of her mouth was . . .

"I'm pissed! What's with those stupid teachers? They had to go and get in my way!"

She was venting while in the bunny outfit. I had a general idea of what happened, but I asked anyway.

"Was there some kind of a problem?"

"Way beyond that! We hadn't even distributed half the flyers when the teachers came running over and told us to stop! Who do they think they are?!"

You know, if two bunny girls start handing out flyers at the front gate, people who aren't even teachers are going to come running to stop you.

"Mikuru started sobbing. I was dragged to the student guidance office. Even that handball moron Okabe was brought in."

The guidance counselor and Okabe the homeroom teacher probably had a hard time figuring out where to put their eyes.

"Anyway, I'm pissed! That's enough for today. Dismissed!"

Haruhi tore the bunny ears from her head and threw them on the floor and began removing the bunny outfit. I quickly ran out of the room.

"How long are you going to keep crying?! Come on, get changed already!"

I leaned against the hallway wall as I waited for them to finish changing. It's not that Haruhi's an exhibitionist. She probably just had no idea what effect their scantily clad bodies had on males. Similarly, she didn't choose the bunny girl costume for its sensuality; she simply thought it would attract attention.

She'll never be able to have a serious relationship.

I really wish she'd start being concerned about guys who may be watching, or at the very least, me. All the stress was wearing me down. I had to hope for some kind of improvement, if only for Asahina's sake. In any case . . . Nagato should really have said something.

Asahina eventually exited the room, staggering and stumbling, looking like a student who had just failed all her tests to get into college for the second year in a row. Not knowing what to say, I remained silent.

"Kyon. . . ."

She sounded like a ghost returning from a fancy cruise ship that had sunk deep into the ocean.

". . . If I become ruined for marriage, will you take me . . . ?"

What should I say? And wait, you're going to call me by that name, too?

Asahina, moving like a robot out of gas, returned my blazer to me. For a moment, I perversely hoped that she would jump into my arms and start sobbing, but she walked off with an expression like rotten, green vegetables.

Kind of a pity.

The next day, Asahina didn't come to school.

The name Haruhi Suzumiya had already been floating around school, but thanks to the bunny mess, her name had transcended mere notoriety into the realm of common knowledge for the entire student body. That was fine with me. I couldn't care less if the whole school knew about Haruhi's eccentric behavior.

The problems were that the name Mikuru Asahina had begun spreading in association with hers and the fact that I felt as though the people around me were giving *me* strange looks.

"Man, Kyon . . . You've finally become one of Suzumiya's merry friends," Taniguchi said in an irritatingly sympathetic tone during break. "I never would have expected Suzumiya to make friends. I guess the world is a crazy place after all."

Shove it.

"Seriously, I was so surprised yesterday. I was going home when I saw bunny girls standing at the front gate. Didn't even have time to wonder if I was dreaming. It made me question if I was losing my sanity."

That was Taniguchi. He was waving a familiar piece of paper around.

"What is this SOS Brigade? What do you do in it?"

Ask Haruhi. I have no idea. Don't want to know either. Even if I did know, I probably wouldn't want to put words to it.

"It says to tell you about mysteries. What exactly does that mean? And I don't really understand this part about how a normal mystery won't do."

Even Ryoko Asakura came over for a bit.

"It looks like you people are having fun. But it would be best if you didn't violate moral sensibilities. That stunt went a bit too far."

I should have skipped school too.

Haruhi was still mad. Not just about the fact that she was interrupted during flyer distribution, but about the fact that a day had passed without a single e-mail arriving at the SOS Brigade address. I was expecting to get one or two prank e-mails, but it looked like the world had more common sense than I thought. I'm positive that was because everyone realized that getting involved with Haruhi would only bring trouble.

Haruhi glared at the empty inbox with a wrinkled brow as she moved the optical mouse around.

"Why haven't we gotten a single e-mail?"

"It's been one day. Maybe there are people with incredible tales of supernatural happenings, but they don't want to tell such a dubious, untrustworthy brigade."

I said that to appease her. In reality . . .

Do you know of any mysterious events? Yes, I do. Oh, that's wonderful. Please tell me about it. I understand. It's like . . .

As if that could ever happen. Listen up, Haruhi. That stuff only happens in comic books or fiction. Reality is far more severe and serious. This little prefectural high school in some random corner of Japan doesn't have any ongoing conspiracies involving the end of the world. There aren't any non-humans wandering around quiet residential areas. There isn't a spaceship buried in the hill behind school. None of this will ever happen. Not a single one of them. You understand, right? The truth is that you actually understand, right? It's just that you have nowhere to vent the frustrations of youth, and that restlessness is leading you down a different path. Snap out of it already. How about you go find some handsome guy and walk home from school together or go see a movie together on Sundays? And join some sports club and knock yourself out. They'd make you a regular member in a flash.

. . . At least, that's what I would have liked to tell her, but I got the feeling I'd be eating Haruhi's fist after about five lines, so I refrained.

"Is Mikuru absent today?"

"She might not ever come back. The poor thing. I hope she wasn't traumatized by the ordeal."

"I even brought a new outfit for her."

"Wear it yourself."

"Of course I'm going to wear it too. But it's no fun when Mikuru isn't here."

Following precedence, Yuki Nagato and her virtually nonexistent presence had become one with the table. There was no reason to be so particular about Asahina. Haruhi could use Nagato as her dress-up doll. Or I guess that's not exactly better. But I got the feeling that unlike the crybaby Asahina, Nagato would calmly put on the bunny outfit as ordered. And I realized I wouldn't mind seeing that.

The long-awaited transfer student had come.

I was informed of this by Haruhi during the short period of time before morning homeroom.

"Don't you think it's amazing? One really came!"

Haruhi was hovering over her desk with a stellar smile like a preschooler receiving a present she'd been waiting for.

I didn't know where she heard it from, but apparently the student was transferring into class 1-9.

"This is a once-in-a-lifetime chance. It's unfortunate that the student isn't in our class, but it's still a mysterious transfer student. No doubt about it."

"How can you tell before you've even seen the student?"

"Didn't I already tell you? Survey says that a student who transfers in halfway through the year is practically guaranteed to be mysterious!"

Just when, by whom, and how was that statistic derived? There's your mystery.

If any student transferring in the month of May can be considered mysterious, then you'd have to assume that Japan has an excess of mysterious transfer students.

However, this trademarked Haruhi theory did not follow common sense. Haruhi took off as soon as first period ended. Probably off to 1-9 to scout the mysterious transfer student.

And right before the bell rang, Haruhi returned with a dour look on her face.

"Was the student mysterious?"

"Hmm . . . Didn't seem that mysterious."

Obviously.

"We talked for a bit, but I don't know enough to be sure yet. Might just be pretending to be a normal student. I'd say that's the more probable scenario. It'd be a waste to reveal your true identity the day you transfer in. I'll go do some more questioning during the next break."

Don't. You probably startled the 1-9 people.

Let's picture it: Haruhi, who's practically never initiated a conversation with anyone, suddenly comes into your classroom and grabs the nearest person. "Which one's the transfer student?" she asks, and the second someone answers, she charges in that direction. Then she probably barges into a happy cluster of friendly students getting acquainted and makes her way to the center, drawing close to the surprised transfer student. "Where did you come from? What's your true identity?" Like a cross-examination.

I thought of something.

"Was it a guy? Or a girl?"

"Could have been disguised. But for now, he looked male."

Then it's a guy.

Which means the SOS Brigade would finally get another male member. He would probably be forced to join no matter what he said, for the sole reason that he was a transfer student. But he might not be as good-natured as Asahina and me. Would things really go so well? No matter how overbearing Haruhi is, a stronger-willed person would probably be able to resist her, right?

If she assembled enough members, we would really have to

make this foolish student association, "The Save the World by Overloading It with Fun Haruhi Suzumiya Brigade" official, huh? Setting aside the matter of whether or not the school would accept it, the person who would have to complete the paperwork would be, ten to one, me. And then I'd be stuck with the label "Haruhi Suzumiya's subordinate" for the next three years.

I hadn't actually thought about what I'd do after graduation, but I somewhat wanted to go to college, so I hoped to avoid doing anything that would be put on my record. But as long as I was with Haruhi, that didn't seem very possible.

What was I going to do?

I couldn't do a thing.

I should have stopped Haruhi and made her disband the SOS Brigade, even if my arms were virtually tied behind my back.

Then I should have soundly lectured Haruhi and convinced her to live a normal life.

Forget about aliens, time travelers, and espers. Find some random guy and put your effort into a relationship, or work out your body on some sports team. I should have forced her to spend the next three years as an ordinary student.

If only I had.

If I had a stronger sense of purpose or will to act, I wouldn't have been washed away by this current called Haruhi Suzumiya and forced to swim in an ocean of idiosyncrasies. The world would have retained its dignity. We would have lived normal lives for three years and then graduated in a normal fashion.

. . . Maybe.

The only reason I say this now is because I experienced things that were anything but normal. If you look at the flow of this story, you should have figured it out already.

Where do I begin?

I guess I'll start around the time when the transfer student came to the club room.

CHAPTER 3

Asahina, after being recognized as one of the two bunny girls, bravely recovered just one day later and showed up at the club after school.

Not that our club had anything to do. I had brought an old Othello board I'd dug up from home and was currently playing a game with Asahina as we chatted.

It was good that we had a homepage up, but seeing that the access counter wasn't going up and we weren't receiving any e-mails, it was pretty much useless. The computer was now used solely for surfing the Internet. This would make those Computer Society guys break down in tears.

Yuki Nagato continued reading silently to the side as Asahina and I began our third round.

"Suzumiya seems to be late," Asahina murmured as she stared at the board.

Her expression didn't look overly downcast. That was a relief. All things considered, being in the same room as a cute girl one year my senior was enough to make my heart flutter.

"A transfer student came today. She probably went off to solicit him."

"Transfer student . . . ?" Asahina tilted her head like a little bird.

"Some guy transferred into 1-9. Haruhi was overjoyed. She must really love transfer students."

Place one black piece. Flip one white piece.

"Hmm...?"

"In any case, Asahina, I'm amazed that you were willing to come back to the club room."

"Well... I was a bit hesitant, but I'd be lying if I said I didn't have my concerns."

Didn't you say something similar before?

"What are you concerned about?"

Click. Pitter patter. Her willowy fingers flipped the pieces.

"Umm... It's nothing."

I suddenly felt something next to me and turned to find Nagato. Her facial expression resembled that of a china doll, as always, but for the first time, I could see glimmers of light in her eyes behind those glasses.

"..."

The look in her eyes reminded me of a newly born kitten seeing a dog for the first time. Her eyes remained glued to my fingers as I placed and flipped pieces.

"Want to take my place, Nagato?"

My question was met with a robotic blink of her eyes and a nod of her head so subtle that you'd have to be looking really hard to notice it. I exchanged positions with Nagato and sat down next to Asahina.

Nagato picked up an Othello piece between two fingers and stared closely at it. Then, as though startled by its completely unanticipated mass and magnetic adhesion to the board, she drew back her hand.

"Nagato, have you ever played Othello?"

She slowly shook her head from left to right.

"Do you know the rules?"

"Negative."

"Well, you see. You're black so you're placing black pieces while trying to surround white pieces. Surrounded white pieces become black. Whoever has more pieces at the end wins."

"Affirmative."

Nagato placed her pieces in an elegant fashion and clumsily began changing her opponent's pieces to her own.

Asahina, with a new opponent, began acting rather strangely. It looked like her fingers were trembling, and she refused to look up. On top of that, she repeatedly snuck glances at Nagato before quickly looking away. It was like she wasn't even paying attention to the game. Black quickly took an advantage across the board.

What was going on? Asahina seemed overly conscious of Nagato. I had no idea why.

The match quickly ended in an overwhelming victory for black, and just when they were about to begin the next match, the root of all our troubles appeared with a new sacrifice in tow.

"Hey, sorry for the wait!"

That would be Haruhi's fundamentally flawed attempt at a greeting as she firmly gripped a male first year's sleeve.

"This is the transfer student from class 1-9 who arrived today and is already making himself useful! His name is . . ."

She cut off at that point directing a look behind her suggesting that he should handle the rest. The captive young man smiled thinly and turned to the three of us.

"Itsuki Koizumi. It's a pleasure to meet you."

A slender guy who had the whole energetic athlete feel to him. A tactful smile. Benign eyes. He was handsome enough that if they took a picture of him in some random pose and stuck it on one of those supermarket flyers, he'd attract a solid group of die-hard fans. He'll probably be pretty popular if he happens to be a nice guy to boot.

"This is the SOS Brigade. I'm the brigade chief, Haruhi Suzumiya. Those three are members number one, number two, and number three. And incidentally, you're the fourth one. Everyone get along now!"

If that's your idea of an introduction, I'd rather you not introduce us at all. The only things established were your name and the transfer student's name.

"I have no problems with joining."

The transfer student, Itsuki Koizumi, said this while maintaining a composed smile on his face.

"But what does this club do?"

If you put one hundred different people in this situation, all one hundred of them would ask this same question, looking for the answer so many people have sought. The same answer which has consistently eluded me. If you managed to find somebody who could explain Fermat's last theorem, he still wouldn't be able to answer this question. If someone out there can explain something he doesn't know anything about, he's got some incredible swindling skills. However, Haruhi wasn't even fazed. In fact, she even had a fearless smile on her face as she looked at us one by one before speaking.

"I'll tell you just what activities the SOS Brigade engages in. Those would be . . ."

She took a deep breath. Was she trying to be dramatic or had she just been waiting to say these words? Whatever the case, Haruhi proceeded to speak the shocking truth.

"To find aliens, time travelers, and espers and to have fun with them!"

I could feel the entire world grinding to a halt.

Just kidding. My reaction was more along the lines of "thought so." But the same couldn't be said for the remaining three people in the room.

Asahina was completely petrified. Her eyes and mouth formed three perfect circles as she stood frozen, staring at Haruhi's blossoming smile. Yuki Nagato wasn't moving either. She stayed motionless with her head tilted towards Haruhi, looking like her batteries had died. I got the impression that her eyes had widened, just a little bit, which was unexpected. I guess even I-have-no-emotions girl was surprised.

Last was Itsuki Koizumi. He was standing with an expression that could be interpreted as a smile either out of bitter mocking or plain surprise. Koizumi was the first to recover.

"Ah, I see."

He sounded like he had just reached some form of enlightenment. After exchanging glances with Asahina and Yuki Nagato, he nodded with an expression of understanding, then voiced an incomprehensible sentiment.

"Just as one would expect from Suzumiya. Very well. I shall join. I hope to have a good time with everyone."

He smiled, showing his white teeth.

Hello? You're going accept that explanation? Were you even listening?

As I stood pondering, he walked over and extended his hand to me.

"I'm Koizumi. Seeing as how I just transferred here, I'm sure I have a lot to learn from you. I hope you'll show me the ropes."

I shook Koizumi's hand.

"Yeah, I'm . . ."

"That's Kyon."

Haruhi dismissively introduced me and moved on. "The cute one over there is Mikuru and four-eyes here is Yuki." After pointing to those two, she looked quite satisfied with herself.

Thud.

There was a dull sound. That was the sound of Asahina hitting her forehead against the Othello board after trying to stand up in a hurry and tripping over her chair.

"Are you OK?"

Asahina responded to Koizumi by shaking her head like a bob-blehead doll and looking up at the transfer student with dazzling eyes. *Meh.* I didn't really like the expression on her face.

". . . Yes," Asahina answered in a voice soft enough to be mistaken for a mosquito speaking, while looking shyly at Koizumi.

"There you have it. We have five members now so the school can't complain about anything!"

I realized Haruhi was saying something.

"All right, SOS Brigade! It's finally time to unveil ourselves to the world! Everyone! Let's join together as one and give it our all!"

What do you mean by unveil?

When I turned to look, I found that Nagato had returned to her customary position and was taking another crack at her hardcover.

You've been arbitrarily included as a member, you know. Are you OK with that?

Haruhi left with Koizumi in tow, saying something about giving him a tour of the school, and Asahina left because she had other things to do, so the only people left in the club room were Yuki Nagato and myself.

I wasn't in the mood for Othello at that point, and there was nothing fun about watching Nagato read, so I opted to go home pronto. I slung my bookbag over my shoulder. Then I spoke to Nagato.

"See ya."

"Did you read the book?"

My legs came to a halt. Yuki Nagato's dark eyes shot straight through me.

"Book. Do you mean that strangely thick hardcover?"

"Yes."

"No, not yet. . . . Should I return it?"

"Not necessary."

Nagato never minces words. One sentence is all she needs.

"Read it today."

She sounded like she didn't actually care.

"As soon as you get home."

Except she sounded rather commanding for someone who didn't care.

Lately, I hadn't read any stories that weren't out of our Japanese textbook, but I figured if she was that serious about it, it must be good enough to recommend to other people.

"I understand."

Once I responded, Nagato returned to her reading.

I furiously pedaled away on my bicycle in the twilight.

After leaving Nagato and returning to my home, I ate dinner and lounged around before returning to my room to peruse the sci-fi novel that had been loaned to me. Or rather, forced on me. The dense ocean of text was making me dizzy. As I flipped through the book wondering if I could possibly finish this monster, a bookmark fell down onto the carpet about halfway through.

A fancy bookmark with floral printing. I casually flipped it over and discovered there was writing on the back.

7 PM. I'll be waiting in the park in front of Kouyou Park Station.

It was written in beautiful handwriting, almost like it was typed. The laconic handwriting did indeed look like it could belong to Nagato. But that would raise a few questions.

I received this book a number of days ago. This 7 PM would mean 7 PM that night, right? Or would 7 PM tonight work? She couldn't possibly have been waiting every night in the park on the off chance that I might see this message, could she? Did she insist that I read it today because she wanted me to finally find the bookmark? But if that was the case, she could have just told me directly in the club room. And I don't see the point in calling me to the park at night.

I checked my watch. Just past 6:45 PM. Kouyou Park is the closest station to our school, but it takes me at least twenty minutes by bike to get there from my house.

I spent no more than ten seconds mulling it over.

I put the bookmark in my jeans pocket, shot out of room and leapt down the stairs like the March Hare. I ran into my sister walking out of the kitchen eating ice cream, answering her "Where are you going, Kyon?" with "The station." I unchained my crappy one-speed bicycle by the entrance, hopped on, and set off, using my foot to flip on the light. Pedaling furiously, I reminded myself to put some air in the tires when I got back.

I'd laugh if Nagato wasn't even there.

Looked like I wouldn't be laughing.

Since I was abiding by traffic safety regulations, it was around 7:10 when I reached the park. It's removed from any major roads so there weren't many people around at that time of night.

With the rush of cars and trains behind me, I pushed my bicycle along as I walked into the park. I barely spotted, next to one of the wooden benches underneath the uniformly placed lamp posts, the faint silhouette of Yuki Nagato.

She seriously had no presence. A stranger casually passing by might take her for a ghost or something.

Nagato noticed me approaching and stood up like a puppet whose strings had been yanked.

She was wearing her uniform.

"Was today OK?" I asked.

Nod.

"Could it be that you've been waiting here every night?"

Nod.

". . . Is it something you can't talk about at school?"

Nod. Nagato stood before me.

"This way."

She walked off. I couldn't hear her footsteps. She moved like a ninja. Seeing as how Nagato was rapidly melting into the darkness the further she got, I had no choice but to quickly follow.

After a few minutes of walking along while I watched her short hair sway in the gentle breeze, we reached a condominium not too far from the station.

"Here."

She input the password into the number pad at the entrance to open the glass door. I parked my bike nearby and followed Nagato to the elevator. Once inside the elevator, Nagato stood silently with an unreadable expression on her face. She just stared at the buttons. We reached the seventh floor.

"So, where are we going?"

Yuki responded as we walked down the corridor of doors. "My home."

I froze in my tracks. Wait a sec. Why was I being invited to Nagato's home?

"Because no one's here."

Holy — wait a sec. What was that supposed to mean?

Nagato opened the door to apartment 708 and stared at me. "Enter."

For real?

Trying my best not to show the consternation I felt, I warily stepped in. I removed my shoes and had taken one step in when the door closed behind me.

It felt like I'd just crossed the point of no return. When I turned around after hearing that ominous sound, I was met by Nagato's stare.

"Go in."

And with that said, Nagato took off her shoes in one swift motion. If it had been completely dark inside the room, I would have dropped everything and run for it, but the large room was filled with the hollow shine of bright light.

Her place had three bedrooms, a kitchen, and a dining room. Factoring in its proximity to the station, it was probably an expensive place.

But still, the room looked utterly devoid of life.

We passed through the living room, which had a tiny table and nothing else. Amazingly enough, there weren't even any curtains up. There wasn't any carpeting on the fifteen square meters or so of light brown wood tiling.

"Sit."

She said this before disappearing into the kitchen. I sat down cross-legged near the table with my back slouched.

As I ran through the possible reasons a teenage girl would bring a teenage boy to her home when her family's out, Nagato placed a tray holding a teapot and teacups on the table, moving like a marionette, before sitting down across from me, still wearing her uniform.

Silence.

She didn't pour the tea. She stared expressionlessly through her glasses, which only served to increase my discomfort.

I figured I needed to say something.

"Ah . . . Where's your family?"

"They aren't here."

"Well, I can see that. Are they out?"

"I am the only one who is ever here."

That was the longest sentence I've heard from Nagato yet.

"You're living alone?"

"Yes."

Aha. A girl who was barely in high school living all alone in such an expensive apartment. Probably some special circumstances there. But yeah, I was relieved I didn't have to meet her parents so soon. Or it was too early to be relieved, wasn't it?

"So what did you want?"

She poured the contents of the teapot into a teacup and placed it before me, almost like an afterthought.

"Drink."

Okay, I guess. I drank the roasted green tea as Nagato watched me the way you would watch a giraffe in the zoo. She wasn't even touching her cup.

Crap, it's poison! . . . Yeah, right.

"Is it good?"

I think that was the first time she'd asked a question.

"Yeah . . ."

The moment I set the empty cup down on the table, Nagato refilled it with more yellowish-brown liquid. Having no real choice, I drank it. Once I finished that, it was instantly refilled a third time. Soon, the teapot was empty, and Nagato stood to go refill it when I stopped her.

"Forget the tea. Could you tell me why you brought me here?"

Nagato, frozen in a half-risen state, returned to her original position in a rewinding fashion. She still didn't open her mouth.

"What is it that you couldn't tell me at school?"

I tried to get her to speak. She finally spread her thin lips.

"About Haruhi Suzumiya."

She gracefully knelt on the floor with her back straight.

"And also, about myself."

She shut her mouth for a moment.

"That is what I need to talk about."

And with that, she fell silent again.

Can't you speed it up or something?

"What about you and Suzumiya?"

That was the first time I'd seen Nagato show emotion on her face. Almost like she was troubled or hesitating. Either way, you'd have to look really closely to notice it. Her expressive face only differed by a few millimeters from her expressionless face.

"It is difficult to convey in words. Discrepancies may arise during the transmission of data. Regardless, listen."

And Nagato began talking.

"Haruhi Suzumiya and I are not ordinary humans."

She was already saying weird stuff.

"I kind of knew that already."

"That isn't what I mean."

Nagato stared at her fingertips crossed on her lap.

"I am not referring to the absence of universally accepted personality traits. I mean what I said. She and I are different from the vast majority of humans like yourself."

"I don't get it."

"A humanoid interface created to make contact with organic life forms by the supervisor of this galaxy, the Data Overmind. That would be me."

". . ."

"My job is to observe Haruhi Suzumiya and report all obtained data to the Overmind."

". . ."

"That is the task I have performed since I was born three years ago. During the past three years, no uncertain elements appeared. The situation was extremely stable. However, recently, an irregular factor which cannot go unheeded has appeared near Haruhi Suzumiya."

". . ."

"That would be you."

"The Data Overmind.

"A data life form possessing no physical body with a high level of intelligence, born from the sea of data which covers the galaxy. Make that the entire universe.

"Initially born as data before congregating with other data and becoming sentient. Evolved by gathering data.

"Possesses no tangible mass, exists only as data, and is impossible to observe through any form of optical measures.

"Has existed since the creation of the universe, magnified in accordance with the expansion of the universe, broadened its database, and developed while growing to enormous proportions.

"Held knowledge of the whole universe since the birth of Earth and this solar system long ago. From the Data Overmind's perspective, this solar system on the edge of the Milky Way held no significant merit. For there were a large number of other planets on which organic life forms occurred.

"However, the third planet in that system was home to the evolution of bipedal organic life forms who developed cognitive ability, which could be considered intelligence, and consequently, Earth, as this oxidized planet is called by its present inhabitant life forms, grew in significance.

"For it was previously believed that organic life forms, possessing unconditionally limited data accumulation and transmission capabilities, could never develop intelligence."

Yuki Nagato said all this with a deathly serious expression on her face.

"The Data Overmind held interest in the life forms categorized as humans that occur on Earth. Perhaps they possessed the potential to break free of the cul-de-sac of autoevolution into which data life forms have fallen.

"Unlike data life forms, which were complete from the genesis stage, humans began as imperfect organic life forms that achieved a rapid rate of autoevolution. They increased their capacity for data retention while creating, processing, and storing new data.

"The emergence of self-awareness among the universe's maldistributed organic life forms was a common phenomenon; however, terrestrial humans were the first instance of evolution to a higher order of intelligence. The Overmind carefully continued thorough observation.

"And three years ago, we observed a data flare unlike any other witnessed on this planet. An explosion of data erupting from the region of a bow-shaped archipelago instantly shrouded the planet and diffused into outer space. At its center was Haruhi Suzumiya.

"Neither cause nor effect is known. The Data Overmind found it impossible to analyze the data. It could only be read as meaningless junk data.

"What's critical is that humans should only be able to handle a limited amount of information, yet only one of those terrestrial humans, Haruhi Suzumiya, was able to trigger a torrent of data.

"Haruhi Suzumiya continues to transmit intermittent torrents of data at completely random intervals. Furthermore, Haruhi Suzumiya herself is unaware of this.

"Over the past three years, a number of inquiries have been performed examining the entity known as Haruhi Suzumiya from all perspectives. However, her true identity remains unknown. Regardless, a sector of the Overmind believes that for humanity and, furthermore, all data life forms, Haruhi Suzumiya is the key to their autoevolution and thus, has commenced analysis accordingly.

"They, as data life forms, are unable to directly communicate with organic life forms, for they possess no language. Humans lack the means to transmit ideas without words. That is why human-purpose interfaces such as myself were created. The Overmind is able to come in contact with humans through me."

Nagato finally lifted her teacup to her lips. Her throat might have been parched after speaking a year's worth of words.

" . . . "

I had nothing to say.

"Haruhi Suzumiya holds hidden potential for autoevolution. It is likely that she possesses the ability to control data in her surrounding environment as she wishes. That is why I am here. Why you are here."

"Hold on." I said this with my mind all a jumble.

"I'll be frank. I have no idea what you're talking about."

"Believe me."

I had never seen such an earnest expression on Nagato's face before.

"The amount of data transmittable through verbal means is limited. I am merely a terminal, an organic interface for contact with humans. My processing facilities are unable to fully convey the Data Overmind's thought process. Please understand."

Easier said than done.

"Why me? Assuming that I believe you're an interface for that Overmind or whatever, then why are you revealing your identity to me?"

"You have been chosen by Haruhi Suzumiya. Whether or not Haruhi Suzumiya is aware of it, her consciousness has an effect on the environment in the form of unconditional data. There must be a reason why you were chosen."

"There isn't."

"There is. You are probably the key to Haruhi Suzumiya. You and Haruhi Suzumiya hold all potential within your grasp."

"Are you serious?"

"Naturally."

I looked extremely hard at Yuki Nagato's face for the first time. Here I was, marveling at how the tight-lipped wonder had finally opened her mouth, and out came this winding freakish spiel. I knew she was odd, but I never would have imagined she was out of her mind.

Data Overmind? Humanoid interface?

My ass.

"Now look here. If you go tell Haruhi this story, she'll be overjoyed. Quite frankly, I don't understand any of this stuff. Sorry."

"A large sector of the Data Overmind has recognized that if Haruhi Suzumiya becomes aware of her own value and ability, there is the potential for indeterminable risks. We must observe the situation for now."

"Isn't it possible that I'll tell Haruhi everything I just heard?"

"Even if you do, she won't take the data you feed her seriously."

She had a point.

"I am not the only interface placed on Earth by the Data Overmind. A sector of the Data Overmind intends on initiating proactive activity and observing the resulting fluctuations in data. You are the key to Haruhi Suzumiya. When crisis approaches, you will be first."

I can't take any more of this.

I prepared to make my leave. "The tea was good. Thanks."

Nagato didn't stop me.

She was staring at the teacup with her customary expression devoid of emotion. She looked a bit lonely, but I was probably just hallucinating.

After answering my mom's inquiry as to where I had gone with some vague reply, I returned to my room. I lay down on my bed and mulled over Nagato's long speech.

If I believed everything Nagato said, that would mean she isn't human. Not even of this world. Long story short, an alien.

A mysterious existence. What Haruhi had been passionately searching for.

And it was right next to her all this time. I guess that's what they mean by "Can't see the forest for the trees."

. . . Ha. Ha. Ha. Retarded.

My eyes fell upon the thick novel I had dropped. I picked it and the bookmark up and stared at its colorful cover before placing it near the head of my bed.

Nagato probably got those bizarre delusions running through her head because she sits alone in her apartment reading these sci-fi books all the time. She probably doesn't talk to anyone in her class either. Just stays in her little shell. Forget your books.

Try to make some friends, even if they're superficial. Just enjoy normal school life. The poker face has to go. She's probably pretty cute when she smiles.

I suppose I'll return the book tomorrow. . . . Well, I might as well read it.

After school the next day.

Since I was on cleaning duty, I was late to the club room and found Haruhi playing with Asahina.

"Stay still! Stop struggling!"

Haruhi had again half-stripped a resisting Asahina.

"Kyaa!"

Asahina screamed upon seeing me enter the room.

I took one look at Asahina standing in just her underwear before taking one step back through the mostly opened door and shutting it.

"Excuse me."

I waited ten minutes. The duet of Asahina's lovely shrieks and Haruhi's shouts of enjoyment came to an end. In its wake, Haruhi spoke. "You can come in now!"

I entered the room and was promptly struck dumb.

A maid stood before me.

Clothed in dress and apron, Asahina, on the verge of tears, sat in a chair and quickly turned to give me a forlorn look.

A white apron and wide-hem flared skirt with blouse. The pristine white stockings had a very fine luster.

A flawless maid.

"Well? Isn't she cute?" Haruhi said proudly, as though she had something to do with it, while patting Asahina's hair.

I can agree with that. I feel sorry for Asahina, sitting dejectedly with a pitiable look on her face, but she looks ridiculously cute.

"Anyway, that's a job well done."

Ignoring the whispered "No, it isn't," from Asahina, I turned to Haruhi.

"What's the point in dressing her up as a maid?"

"When it comes to turn-ons, you can't forget about maids."

Again, I have no idea what she's talking about.

"I thought hard on this matter."

You only think about things that are better left alone.

"Stories set in a school always have an alluring character present. In other words, stories begin wherever an alluring character is present. You could say it's inevitable. Understand? Mikuru is a Lolita and a timid person and also possesses an important element of turn-ons, being well-endowed. If you put her into a maid outfit on top of all that, her turn-on factor will jump up like crazy. Anyone can see that she'll set records for turning on people. It's like we've already won."

What are you trying to win?

While I was basically struck speechless, Haruhi had gotten her hands on a digital camera and was saying something about taking pictures to commemorate.

Asahina, face flaming red, shook her head.

"Don't take pictures. . . ."

You can get on your knees and pray or whatever. If Haruhi says it will be so, then it must be so.

Haruhi forced the entreating Asahina into a number of poses as the flash went off over and over.

"Ahh . . ."

"Look this way. Tilt the chin a bit. Clutch the apron. That's it. Bigger smile!"

Haruhi relentlessly took pictures as she rattled out commands. When I asked her where she got the digital camera from, she said that she borrowed it from the photography club. Isn't it almost certain that she swiped it?

During this photo shoot, Yuki Nagato sat in her usual spot,

engaged in her usual activity of reading. She said a lot of crazy stuff yesterday, but she was as tight-lipped as ever today. I was somehow relieved.

"Kyon, take over as cameraman."

Haruhi handed me the digital camera and turned towards Asahina. She grabbed Asahina's little shoulders the way an alligator would creep up on water fowl.

"Haha. . . ."

Haruhi smiled kindly at the scrunched-up Asahina.

"Mikuru. Let's make you a little sexier."

The moment she said that, Haruhi removed the ribbon from the bodice of the maid outfit. She then quickly unbuttoned three buttons to reveal cleavage.

"Hey! No . . . What are you . . ."

"It's fine! It's fine!"

How is this fine?

Asahina was then forced to place her hands on her knees and lean forward. I had to avert my eyes from the ample valley of her chest, a mismatch with her petite body and baby face. Except that if I averted my eyes, I couldn't take pictures, so I was forced to look through the finder.

I repeatedly pressed the shutter per Haruhi's orders.

Cheeks flushed with embarrassment as she was forced into poses accentuating her chest, Asahina awkwardly smiled at the camera, her eyes watering close to tears. She was oozing incomparable charm.

Crap. I think I'm in love.

"Yuki, lend me your glasses."

Nagato slowly looked up from her book, slowly removed her glasses, handed them to Haruhi, and slowly went back to reading. She could read without glasses?

Haruhi placed the glasses on Asahina's face.

"It looks good when they're slightly slipping off. Yeah, it's perfect! A Lolita with shapely breasts in a maid outfit wearing glasses! It's magnificent! Kyon, keep taking pictures!"

I wasn't refusing to take pictures, but what were all these pictures of Asahina dressed as a maid going to be used for?

"Mikuru, from now on, wear these clothes when in the club room."

"You can't be serious. . . ."

Asahina did her best to voice her objection, but Haruhi continued.

"'Cause it's so cute! Man, even a girl like me can't help herself!"

She grabbed Asahina and rubbed her face against hers. Asahina cried out while struggling to escape before finally succumbing to Haruhi's will.

Hey, now. I'm getting pretty envious here, Haruhi. Or, like, yeah, I should be stopping her.

"That's enough now, Haruhi."

I grabbed the back of Haruhi's neck as she continued her open sexual harassment of Asahina. I was having a hard time pulling her away.

"Hey. Cut it out already!"

"What's wrong? You can do perverted things to Mikuru, too."

A fine idea. But seeing as how Asahina was rapidly turning pale, I could not offer my consent.

"Whoa. What is this?"

That would be Itsuki Koizumi, standing in the doorway, his bag in hand, watching us struggling.

He looked curiously at Haruhi, trying to thrust her hand down Asahina's open dress, me, holding back that hand, Asahina, trembling in her maid outfit, and Nagato, calmly reading without her glasses.

"Is this some kind of game?"

"Koizumi. Great timing. Let's all have fun with Mikuru!"

What the hell are you saying?

The corners of Koizumi's mouth turned upwards. If he expressed assent, I'd have to treat him as an enemy.

"I'll pass. I'm scared of what will happen afterward."

He set his bag on the table and took one of the chairs propped against the wall and unfolded it.

"May I sit in and observe?"

He sat down and crossed his legs, looking at me with an amused face.

"Don't mind me. Please continue."

You've got it wrong. I'm helping her, not assaulting her.

Confusion over with, I managed to get between Haruhi and Asahina. As Asahina weakly collapsed backward, I hurried over to support her. I was surprised by how light she was as I guided her to a chair. The sight of Asahina exhausted in her disheveled maid outfit was, quite honestly, extremely hot.

"Oh, well. We already took a bunch of pictures."

Haruhi removed the glasses from the beautiful face of Asahina, her body slouched back with her eyes closed, and returned them to Nagato.

Nagato took the glasses and placed them back on her face wordlessly. As though her long speech yesterday was some kind of lie. Maybe it was just a lie. Some kind of elaborate joke.

"Now, let's commence the first SOS Brigade meeting!"

Haruhi loudly proclaimed that out of the blue while standing atop the brigade chief chair. Where'd that come from?

"We've done a lot to make it this far. We passed out flyers, and we even made a homepage. The celebrity of the SOS Brigade in this school has skyrocketed. The first stage can be considered a huge success."

How can you call emotionally scarring Asahina a huge success?

"However, not a single tale of mysterious happenings has reached our brigade's e-mail inbox, and not a single student has come in for consultation regarding bizarre troubles."

That's 'cause fame isn't enough to do it. Nobody has a clue as to what this club does yet. Most importantly, the school doesn't even recognize us as a club.

"Someone once said, 'Good things come to those who wait.' However, we live in the modern world now. You have to find good things for yourself, even if it means digging them out of the ground. That's why we're going to go search!"

Nobody else was interjecting, so I did. ". . . For what?"

"The mysteries of this world! If we search every corner of the city, at least one mysterious phenomenon is bound to pop out!"

I would say that your mind is the far bigger mystery.

Completely ignoring the disbelief on my face, the enigmatic smile suggesting little consideration on Koizumi's face, the absence of emotion on Nagato's face, and the helpless look of resignation to what fate might bring on Asahina's face, Haruhi waved her arms around and shouted.

"This Saturday! In other words, tomorrow! Meet at 9 AM in front of Kitaguchi Station. Don't be late. If you don't show, heads will roll!"

Heads will roll, huh?

If you're wondering what Haruhi planned on doing with the pictures of Asahina in a maid outfit, it was revealed that the damn girl was going to put the pictures in that digital camera on my half-assed Web site.

I noticed this after Haruhi had finished placing a dozen of those pictures in a row on the top page, all set to greet visitors, mere seconds before she was going to upload them into cyberspace.

This would jump the dead access counter up to five digits in a flash.

Are you an idiot?

I had to draw the line here as I desperately stopped Haruhi and deleted the pictures. If Asahina found out that those unbecoming pictures of her in the maid costume in knockout poses had been spread around the world, she'd definitely faint on the spot.

Oddly enough, Haruhi quietly looked at me as I fervently lectured her, but I can't be sure if she understood what I meant by the dangers of putting personal information that may reveal your identity on the Internet.

"I get it," she said sullenly before consenting to delete them. In this case, I probably should have deleted all the pictures, but that would be a waste. I created a hidden folder on the hard drive, stored the pictures there, and set a password instead.

I'll save them for my private viewing pleasure.

CHAPTER 4

Meet at 9 AM on a day off? Screw that.

And with that in mind, I pedaled away on my bicycle toward the station, bemoaning how pathetic I was.

Kitaguchi Station is located in the center of the city and is also a central terminal for the train system. On weekends, it tends to be packed with bored young people. Most of them are on their way to larger cities. The only place to go around the station would be the shopping mall. It's still a big enough crowd to make me think about how each person in the mob has his or her own individual life.

I illegally (sorry) parked my bike in front of the closed bank and reached the north ticket gate five minutes before nine. Everyone had already gathered in silence.

"Late. Penalty!" she said, looking at me.

"I got here before nine."

"Doesn't matter if you weren't late. The last person here gets penalized. That's my rule."

"News to me."

"'Cause I just came up with it," Haruhi said with a cheerful look on her face, wearing a long, brand-name T-shirt and a knee-length denim skirt. "So buy everyone something to drink."

Haruhi, standing with her hands on her hips in casual attire, felt a hundred times more approachable than when she was in the classroom with a sour look on her face. Bemused, I ended up nodding. Following Haruhi's instructions to decide on a plan of action for the day, we headed toward the café.

Asahina was dressed in a white sleeveless one-piece dress with a light blue cardigan over it. Her hair was gathered in the back by a barrette, and the way it made her hair bounce up and down as she walked was quite charming. Her smile had the air of a little lady dressing like an adult. She also carried a fashionable purse.

Koizumi stood next to me dressed quite formally in a pink shirt with a brown sports jacket. He even had a dark red tie on. Kind of depressing, but I have to admit he looked sharp. Plus he's taller than me.

Yuki Nagato silently brought up the end of the line wearing her familiar sailor uniform. It seemed like she'd been completely turned into an SOS Brigade member, but wasn't she supposed to be in the literary club? After hearing that crazy speech in her quiet apartment the other day, I was even more concerned about the lack of expression on her face. But why was she wearing her uniform on a day off?

Our puzzling group of five entered the café through the revolving door and sat in the back. We gave our respective orders to the waitress, except for Nagato, who stared at the menu with unfathomable intensity — but without any expression on her face — and couldn't seem to make up her mind. After enough time had passed to have made a cup of instant ramen . . .

"Apricot," she announced.

I'm the one paying anyway.

This was Haruhi's plan:

We would now split up into two groups and search the city. If one group found any mysterious phenomena, it was to contact the other group via cell phone while continuing the search. Then regroup at the meeting spot and discuss what to do next.

That was all.

"Let's draw for it then."

Haruhi took five toothpicks from the container on the table, marked two of them with a pen she borrowed from the café, and held them toward us with only the heads sticking out for us to draw. I drew marked. Asahina also drew marked. The other three drew unmarked.

"Hmm, so these are the groups...."

For some reason, Haruhi alternated glares between Asahina and me before sticking her nose in the air.

"Kyon. This isn't a date. Be serious about it. Understand?"

"I know."

I guess I was looking a little pleased with myself. Lucky me. Asahina held one hand against her flushed cheeks as she gazed at the tip of her toothpick. Excellent. Excellent indeed.

"What exactly should we be looking for?" Koizumi asked rather blithely. Next to him was Nagato, who was periodically moving her cup to her mouth.

Haruhi slurped up the last few drops of her iced coffee before brushing her hair behind her ear.

"Anything that defies common sense. Anything that looks suspect. Any person that seems mysterious. Yes, discovering the location of a distortion in space-time, or an alien masquerading as a human would be good."

I almost spit out the mint tea in my mouth. Oh? Asahina had a similar expression next to me. Nagato looked the same as always, though.

"I see," Koizumi said.

Do you really understand?

"So basically, we should search for actual aliens, time travelers, and espers or any signs they may have left behind. I understand perfectly." Koizumi's face looked rather cheerful.

"Yes! You show promise, Koizumi. That's exactly right. Kyon, you should learn to be as understanding as he is."

Don't feed his ego too much. Koizumi returned my hateful glare with a smile.

"Then shall we get going?"

Leaving the bill in my hand, Haruhi strode out of the café.

I don't remember how many times I've said this already, but I'll say it again:

"Good grief."

With a "This seriously isn't a date! If you go off somewhere to play, I'll strangle you!" for a farewell, Haruhi marched off with Koizumi and Nagato following behind her. Using the station as a base, the Haruhi team went east, while Asahina and I were supposed to search west. Search for what?

"What do we do?"

Asahina held her purse as she watched the other three leave before looking up at me. I wanted to take her home with me right then. I pretended to think it over.

"Hmm. Well, there's no point in standing here, so why don't we just walk around somewhere?"

"OK."

She obediently followed me. The way she quickly jumped away when our shoulders accidentally brushed as she hesitantly walked alongside me painted quite the picture of innocence.

We walked north along a nearby riverbed for no particular reason. The cherry trees would have been pink with petals a month ago, but now there was just a disheartening riverside path.

The place was perfect for strolling along the river, so we passed a number of families and couples. From a stranger's point of view, we would have looked to be a close pair of lovers. They wouldn't expect us to be a couple of fools on a search who don't even know what they're looking for.

"This is the first time I've ever walked around like this."

"Like this?"

"All alone with a boy . . ."

"That's very surprising. You've never gone out with someone before?"

"I haven't."

"Really? But you probably have guys asking you out all the time."

"Well . . ." She hung her head shyly. "But I can't. I'm not allowed to get involved with anyone. At least, not in this . . ."

She suddenly became quiet. Three couples looking like they didn't have a care in the world passed behind us before she spoke again.

"Kyon?"

I was counting the number of leaves floating by in the river when her voice brought me back to the real world.

Asahina looked at me with a brooding expression on her face. She then spoke in a firm voice.

"I have something to tell you."

I could see the determination glimmering in her doe eyes.

She sat next to me on a bench under the cherry trees. But she was finding it hard to start talking. After mumbling things like "Where do I start," "I'm terrible at explaining things," and "You might not believe me," Asahina eventually caught herself and said this.

"I do not belong in this epoch. I come from further into the future."

"I can't tell you exactly when and which time plane I come from. I couldn't tell you if I wanted to. The information about the future that can be revealed to people in the past is severely restricted. I was required to undergo mental conditioning and receive mandatory hypnotism before boarding the trans-time vehicle. So if I try to say anything beyond what's necessary, I will automatically be blocked. Please keep that in mind as you listen."

Asahina spoke.

"Time cannot be viewed as something that flows continuously. Rather, time is an accumulation of punctuated planes."

"I'm already lost."

"Um, let's see. Picture it as animation. It looks like it's moving, but it's actually composed of a sequence of still frames. Time can be considered a similar kind of digital phenomena. Would it be easier to understand if I compare it to a flip book?

"Breaks exist between one time and another time, though their rate of occurrence is close to zero. That is why time appears to have no breaks in continuity.

"Time travel means moving in a three-dimensional direction across the accumulated time planes. Being from the future, my presence on this time plane is similar to that of an extra picture added into a flip book.

"Because time has no continuity, even if I tried to change history in this epoch, those changes wouldn't be reflected in the future. The changes would only affect up to the end of this time plane. If you only scribble on one part of a flip book with hundreds of pages, the story won't change, right?

"Time isn't analog like this river. Every moment is a digital phenomenon made up of accumulated time planes. Do you understand now?"

I considered if I should press my hand against my forehead. I ended up doing it.

Time plane. Digital. I didn't care too much about those things. But a time traveler?

Asahina stared at the edge of her sandals.

"The reason I came to this time plane was because . . ."

A couple with two children passed by, their shadows falling across us.

"It was three years ago. A large timequake was detected. Oh, um. Three years ago if you count from the current time. Back around when you and Suzumiya became middle school students. After arriving in the past to investigate the matter, we were shocked. No matter what we tried, we were unable to go any further back in time."

Again with the three years ago business, huh?

"The conclusion was that a large time fault had appeared between time planes. But we couldn't figure out why the fault was limited to this epoch. We only learned the possible reason recently. . . . Ah, recently for the future I come from."

". . . And the reason is?" Don't tell me it's that.

Unfortunately, my wish wasn't granted.

"Suzumiya."

Asahina said the dreaded word.

"We found her in the center of the time warp. Don't ask how we discovered this. It goes into classified information so I'm unable to explain any further. But it is certain. Suzumiya was the one who sealed the path to the past."

"I really don't think that Haruhi is capable of something like that. . . ."

"We didn't think so either. Truth be told, we are still unable to explain how a single human was able to interfere with time planes. It is a mystery. And Suzumiya is unaware that she's doing any of this. She has no idea that she was the origin of a timequake. I was sent to observe if any new time variations will appear near Suzumiya. . . . Um, I can't think of a good word for it, but it's like surveillance."

". . ." was my response.

"You probably don't believe any of this."

"Not exactly . . . But why are you telling me this?"

"Because you are the person chosen by Suzumiya."

Asahina turned her whole upper body toward me.

"The details are classified so I can't explain any further. However, you are probably an important person to Suzumiya. Every action she performs has a reason behind it."

"Nagato and Koizumi are . . ."

"Those people are extremely similar to me. I never would have expected Suzumiya to assemble us in such a precise fashion."

"Do you know what they are, Asahina?"

"That's classified information."

"What happens if Haruhi is just left alone?"

"That's classified."

"And wait, if you're from the future, you should know what's going to happen."

"That's classified."

"What will happen if I tell Haruhi everything?"

"That's classified."

". . ."

"I'm sorry. I can't tell you. Especially since I don't have enough authority right now." Asahina looked apologetic with a downcast look on her face. "It's OK if you don't believe me. I just wanted to let you know."

I just heard something similar a few days ago. In that empty, silent apartment room.

"I'm sorry. . . ."

Perhaps seeing my silence and worried about what I was thinking, Asahina's eyes became clouded.

". . . About suddenly telling you all this."

"I don't really mind. . . ."

First, there was someone telling me she was an artificial human of alien creation, now a time traveler shows up? How am I supposed to believe all of this? Feel free to let me know.

As I placed my hand on the bench, I happened to touch Asahina's hand. Our pinkies barely touched yet she tore her hand away like she'd been shocked. She looked down again.

We continued to watch the river in silence.

An unknown amount of time passed.

"Asahina."

"Yes . . . ?"

"Can we put this all on hold? Just set the matter of whether or not I believe you aside and put this on hold."

"OK."

Asahina smiled. A brilliant smile.

"That's fine. For now. Please continue to act normally around me. I'm counting on you."

Asahina placed three fingers on the bench and bowed deeply. That's a bit excessive.

"May I ask one thing?"

"What is it?"

"Please tell me your real age."

"That's classified information."

She smiled mischievously.

Afterward, we just meandered around town. Haruhi had firmly reminded me that this wasn't a date, but I really couldn't care less after what I had just heard. We window shopped around some trendy boutiques, bought some soft serve to eat as we walked, browsed through stalls with used women's accessories. . . . In other words, we spent the time doing things a normal couple would do.

If we had held hands on top of that, I could have died and gone to heaven.

My cell phone rang. The caller was Haruhi.

"Reassemble at noon in front of the station like earlier."

She hung up. I checked my watch. 11:50. We couldn't make it in time.

"Suzumiya? What did she say?"

"We're supposed to reassemble, apparently. We'd best hurry."

I wondered how Haruhi would react if we showed up arm in arm. She'd probably be pissed.

Asahina buttoned up her cardigan as she curiously looked up at me.

"Results?"

After we got there ten minutes late, this was the first thing out of Haruhi's mouth. She looked to be in a bad mood.

"Anything?"

"Nothing."

"Were you even looking? Are you sure you weren't just wandering around? Mikuru?"

Asahina shook her head.

"What about you? Did you find anything?"

Haruhi fell silent. Behind her, Koizumi had a cool look on his face and Nagato stood blankly.

"Let's have lunch and plan for the afternoon."

You want to keep going?

As we were eating lunch at a hamburger place, Haruhi told us to split into groups again. She pulled out the five toothpicks she had taken from the café. Resourceful gal.

Koizumi quickly drew his.

"I drew unmarked again."

Sickeningly white teeth. I got the feeling he never stopped smiling.

"Me too."

Asahina showed me the toothpick she drew.

"What about you, Kyon?"

"Marked, unfortunately."

Haruhi directed Nagato to draw a toothpick with an increasingly irritated expression on her face.

As a result of the drawing, I ended up with Nagato and the other three were together.

"..."

Haruhi glared at her unmarked toothpick the way you would glare at a bitter enemy. She then looked at me, then Nagato, munching away at a cheeseburger, and puckered her lips like a pelican's bill.

What is she trying to say?

"Meet in front of the station at four. You had better find something this time."

She noisily slurped down the rest of her shake.

This time, we split up searching north and south. Nagato and I were responsible for the south side. Asahina waved her small hand at me before she went on her way. It made me feel all warm and fuzzy inside.

And so there I was, standing amidst the early afternoon bustle in front of the station.

"What do we do?"

"..."

Nagato was silent.

"Want to get going?"

Once I started walking, she followed suit. I was starting to grow accustomed to how to deal with her.

"Nagato, about what you said the other day . . ."

"What?"

"I've started to feel a little like I can believe you."

"I see."

"Yeah."

"..."

We continued to walk around the station in silence with a hollow atmosphere in pursuit.

"Don't you have any normal clothes?"

"..."

"What do you usually do on days off?"

"..."

"Are you having fun right now?"

"..."

Well, that's pretty much how it went.

This pointless walking around was starting to get on my nerves, so I took Nagato to the library. The main library was closer to the seashore, but there was a new library near the station that had been constructed on land developed during a government expansion project. I don't really borrow books so I've never been inside.

I was planning on sitting down for a break if there was a sofa or something, but while there were sofas, they were all taken. Damn bored people. Don't you have somewhere else to go?

As I looked around the library, discouraged, Nagato floated toward the bookshelves like a sleepwalker. I'll leave her alone.

I used to read a lot. In my early elementary school days, I would read every children's book my mother borrowed from the library from front to back. The books were of varying genres, but I recall that I found them all interesting. Yet I don't remember any of them in detail.

When was it? That I stopped reading. Lost interest in reading?

I drew from the bookshelf whichever book my eyes happened to fall upon and flipped through the pages before placing it back on the shelf and repeating the process. I didn't think that with so many books it would be so hard to find one that looked interesting without having prior knowledge about it. And with such thoughts in mind, I wandered the shelves for a book.

When I looked for Nagato, I spotted her standing in front of a bookshelf near the wall reading a book so thick it could serve as a dumbbell. She must really love thick books.

I spotted some old guy who had been flipping through the sports page getting up from a sofa, so I slipped into the open spot with a randomly selected novel in hand.

It's pretty futile to try to read a book you don't actually want to read, and I soon found myself battling an inevitable onslaught of drowsiness. I quickly fell against the overwhelming waves of enemy attacks and drifted off.

My back pocket vibrated.

"Wha —?"

I jumped up. When the other people looked pointedly at me, I recalled that I was in a library. I wiped the drool off my chin and jogged outside.

I placed the cell phone with its vibration mode in full action to my ear.

"Do you realize what time it is now, you moron?!"

A deafening voice pierced my eardrums. That cleared up my head.

"Sorry, I just woke up."

"What? You lazy bum!"

You're the one person I don't want calling me a dumbass.

I checked my watch. 4:30. We were supposed to meet up at four, I think.

"Get your ass back here! Within thirty seconds!"

Don't be ridiculous.

After she rudely hung up on me, I put my cell phone back in my pocket and walked back into the library. Nagato was easy to find. She was standing still in front of the first bookshelf I spotted, reading some encyclopedia-like book.

This was when the struggle began. In order to move Nagato, who when reading is apparently rooted to the floor, I had to get her a library card so she could borrow the book. All the while ignoring the flood of calls from Haruhi.

When Nagato (carefully holding a philosophy book penned by somebody with a complicated name) and I got back to the station, we were met by three people with three different reactions.

Asahina, looking exhausted, sighed a smile at us. Koizumi shrugged in an exaggerated motion. Haruhi looked like she had just chugged a bottle of Tabasco sauce.

"Late. Penalty." she said.

My treat again, huh?

In the end, after yielding no results or satisfaction and wasting time and money like no one's business, today's outdoor activity came to a close.

"I'm exhausted. Suzumiya walked really fast. It was all I could do to keep up," Asahina said before taking a breath, just as we were splitting up. She then got on her tiptoes and whispered into my ear.

"Thank you for listening to what I had to say today."

She quickly backed off and smiled shyly. Does everybody in the future smile so gracefully?

With a cute "bye" by way of farewell, Asahina walked off. Koizumi lightly patted my shoulder.

"Today was quite fun. Indeed, Suzumiya is every bit the interesting person I expected. I regret that I was unable to be in a group with you today. Perhaps another time."

Koizumi also left with that aggravating, easy smile of his. Nagato had vanished long ago.

Which left Haruhi, glaring at me.

"What exactly were you doing today?"

"Beats me. What exactly was I doing?"

"That kind of mindset won't do!"

It looks like she's seriously pissed.

"Then what about you? Did you discover anything interesting?"

Haruhi bit her lower lip with a light grunt. She might have bitten her lip off if I hadn't said something.

"Well, they're not careless enough to let you find them in one day."

Haruhi glanced at me after my follow-up before quickly turning away.

"The day after tomorrow, we'll hold a review of today's behavior."

She then turned around and walked off without looking back once, quickly blending into the crowd.

I figured I should also get going and headed to the bank, only to find that my bike wasn't there. Instead, there was a sign saying YOUR ILLEGALLY PARKED BICYCLE HAS BEEN CONFISCATED on a nearby lamppost.

CHAPTER 5

A new week began. We'd reached the point where the humidity of the rainy season left us sweating early in the morning. If some guy runs for office on the platform of installing an escalator on this hill, I'd be willing to vote for him — once I'm old enough to vote.

I was sitting in the classroom using a pencil board to fan my neck when oddly enough, Haruhi showed up right before the bell rang.

She dropped her bag on her desk with a plop.

"Fan me too."

"Fan yourself."

Haruhi was jutting her lips out with the same sour look on her face she had when I last saw her two days ago. And I had just been thinking about how her expressions had started to look normal, but instead, she went back to the way she was.

"Look here, Suzumiya. Have you ever heard the song 'Bluebird of Happiness'?"

"What about it?"

"Nothing really."

"Then shut your mouth."

Haruhi glared in some upward sideways direction, I turned to the front of the room, and teacher-man Okabe walked in and started homeroom.

I spent the class period being pressured from behind by Haruhi's depressing aura of displeasure. Man, the bell signaling the end of class had never sounded so divine. Like a field mouse sensing an impending bushfire, I scurried to the safety of the club room.

The sight of Nagato reading in the club room had become the default backdrop. It was like she was an irremovable fixture in the room.

Which is why I spoke to Koizumi, who had arrived just before me.

"Don't you also have something to tell me concerning Suzumiya?"

Only three people are in the room. Haruhi's on cleaning duty this week and Asahina hasn't showed up yet.

"Oh? The 'also' would imply that the other two ladies have already approached you."

Koizumi took a glance at Nagato, who had her head buried in the book she borrowed from the library. I really can't stand how he sounds like he knows everything.

"Let's move to a different location. We wouldn't want Suzumiya to walk in on us."

Koizumi led me to one of the outdoor cafeteria tables. On the way there, he bought coffee from a vending machine and handed it to me. Two guys sitting at a round table is kind of, you know. I guess it couldn't be helped in this case.

"How much do you know?"

"The fact that Suzumiya isn't an ordinary person, I guess."

"That makes things quite simple. That is exactly the case."

Is this some kind of joke? All three of the other SOS Brigade members are making it sound like Haruhi isn't human. Maybe the heat from global warming has gotten to their heads?

"Why don't you start by telling me your true identity?" I asked.

I'm already acquainted with an alien and a time traveler.

"You're not going to tell me you're actually an esper, right?"

"I would rather you not preempt my words."

Koizumi swirled the contents of his paper cup.

"It isn't quite the same. But yes, I would be closest to what you call an esper. Yes, I am an esper."

I drank my coffee in silence. I shouldn't have put in so much sugar. It was too sweet.

"I actually wasn't intending on a sudden transfer to this school, but the situation changed. Surely, I couldn't have anticipated that the two of them would join forces with Haruhi Suzumiya so readily. Up until that point, they had merely observed her from a distance."

Don't talk about Haruhi like she's some kind of rare insect.

Maybe he noticed my narrowed eyebrows.

"Please don't think ill of me. We are doing everything we can. We mean Suzumiya no harm. In fact, we are trying to protect her from possible danger."

"You say we. Which means there are a lot more like you? Espers or whatever."

"I wouldn't say there are a lot, but there are quite a few of us. I'm part of the outer circle so I can't say for sure, but there are probably ten or so around the world. All of them should belong to the Agency."

Now we have an Agency, huh?

"Its composition is unknown. Same goes for the number of members. Though it appears that the top people call the shots."

"...And so, what does this secret organization, the Agency, do?"

Koizumi wet his lips with the lukewarm coffee.

"It's as you imagine. Ever since the beginning of the Agency three years ago, its top priority has been the observation of Haruhi Suzumiya. To put it simply, it was an organization created for the sole purpose of observing Suzumiya. You've probably already guessed as much after hearing what I've said, but I am not the only member of the Agency in this school. There are a number of agents planted here. I have merely come as additional personnel."

Taniguchi's face suddenly popped up in my mind. He said that he'd been in the same class as Haruhi since middle school. Could he possibly be one of Koizumi's people, I asked.

Koizumi quickly dodged that question. "Well, I don't know about that."

"In any case, I can assure you that a number of people are situated near Suzumiya."

Why does everyone like Haruhi so much? She's an eccentric, bossy, self-centered girl who causes trouble for everyone around her. How does she warrant the attention of some grandiose organization? I do have to admit she's easy on the eyes, though.

"I don't know what happened three years ago. All I know is that on that day, I discovered within me what could only be described as ESP. I was in a panic at first. And quite frightened as well. The Agency soon took me in and gave me guidance. Otherwise, I might have been left thinking that I had gone insane and killed myself."

"Sure you haven't actually been insane this whole time?"

"Yes, that possibility cannot be ruled out. However, we fear a more frightening possibility." Koizumi swallowed his self-mocking smile with his coffee and looked surprisingly serious. "When do you believe this world came into existence?"

The conversation had just taken a huge leap in scope.

"Didn't it start with the Big Bang explosion a long time ago?"

"That is the current belief. However, we are unable to discount the hypothesis that the world began three years ago."

I stared back at Koizumi's face. He can't be sane.

"That's impossible. I remember things that happened over three years ago, and my parents are alive and well. I still have the three stitches from when I fell into a ditch as a kid. And what about all that Japanese history I'm cramming into my head?"

"What if I were to say that all humans, including you, had been born one day with those memories intact? How could you confirm or deny that? It doesn't have to be three years ago. If I were to say that the entire universe had been predefined and this world was born a mere five minutes ago, you would find it impossible to formulate an argument to prove me wrong."

". . ."

"For example, take virtual reality. Electrodes are placed into your brain. If the images you see, the air you smell, and the table you feel are all just data being directly transmitted to your brain, you would never realize that they weren't real, would you? In reality, this world is quite fragile."

". . . Let's assume everything you said is true. The world began three years ago or five seconds ago. How do you twist it so Haruhi's name comes up?"

"The higher-ups in the Agency believe that this world is but a dream a certain being is having. We — no — the whole world is but a dream to that being. And because it is just a dream, creating and altering this world we call reality is mere child's play for that being. And we know the name of the being who is capable of such acts."

Maybe it's because he's speaking calmly in formal language, but the expression on his face looks irritatingly mature.

"A being who can create and destroy at will — humans have defined such a being as God."

Hey, Haruhi. You've even got people calling you God now. Whatcha gonna do?

"Which is why the members of the Agency are considerably frightened. If by any chance this world loses the favor of God, it could simply be destroyed and recreated at whim. Like a child who doesn't like how her sand castle looks. This world may be filled with inconsistencies, but I happen to feel some attachment to it. That is why I am assisting the Agency."

"Why don't you just ask Haruhi? Ask her politely not to destroy the world. She might listen to you."

"Of course, Suzumiya is unaware of what she actually is. She has yet to realize her true potential. In that case, we are of the idea that she would be better off not knowing and living out her life in peace."

Koizumi finally went back to his usual smile.

"You could consider her an incomplete god. She is still unable to control the world at will. But while her abilities are still undeveloped, we have begun witnessing signs."

"How can you tell?"

"Why do you think espers such as ourselves and characters such as Mikuru Asahina and Yuki Nagato exist in this world? Because Suzumiya wished for it."

If there are any aliens, time travelers, sliders, or espers here, come join me.

Haruhi's words of introduction in the classroom when I first met her replayed in my mind.

"She is still unable to consciously wield her godlike powers. She can only use them unconsciously through coincidence. However, we know that during these past few months, Haruhi has clearly been displaying powers beyond human comprehension. I probably don't need to tell you the consequences. Suzumiya met Mikuru Asahina and Yuki Nagato, and I was also added to her little group."

"I'm the only one left out?"

"Not exactly. Quite the contrary, you are the biggest mystery. Although it's bad form, I investigated a number of things concerning you. I can assure you, you possess no special abilities. You are an ordinary human."

"Should I be relieved or disappointed?"

"I wouldn't know. It's quite possible that you hold the fate of the world in your hands. This is a request from us to you. Please take care not to let Suzumiya lose all hope for this world."

"If Haruhi is God," I offered, "why don't you capture her and dissect her and figure out how her brain is wired? It might be a quick way to figure out how her world works."

"There are, in fact, diehards within the Agency who advocate such a measure," Koizumi readily assented. "However, the majority is of the opinion that we should not interfere. If we inadvertently sour her mood, there is a high probability that the situation will become irreparable. We wish to preserve the current state of the world, so our only wish is for Suzumiya to live a peaceful life. If we make a mistake, it would be like trying to take roasted chestnuts off an open fire; you'll only end up getting burned."

"So what exactly are we supposed to do?"

"I do not know."

"If theoretically, just theoretically, Haruhi were to suddenly die, what would happen to the world?"

"Indeed. Perhaps the world would be terminated at the same time. Or perhaps the world would continue Godless. Or perhaps a new God would be born. Nobody knows the answer. Not until it happens."

The coffee in my paper cup had grown cold. No longer wanting to drink it, I pushed it to the edge of the table.

"You said you were an esper, right?"

"Yes. We call ourselves by a different name, but simply put, that wouldn't be inaccurate."

"So show me some kind of power. Then I'll believe what you say. For example, reheat this cup of coffee."

Koizumi looked amused as he smiled. I think that was the first time his smile hadn't looked artificial.

"I'm quite sorry, but that's impossible. My power cannot be so easily manipulated. Also, I usually hold no power at all. A number of conditions must be met before I can use my power. I'm sure there will be an opportunity to show you."

He then said, "Sorry to drag on so long. I'll excuse myself for today," and cheerfully left the table.

I watched Koizumi's back until he was out of sight as he lightly walked off. Then I had the sudden idea to pick up the paper cup.

It goes without saying that the contents were cold.

When I returned to the clubroom, I found Asahina standing in her underwear.

". . ."

Asahina held the frilly dress and apron in her hands as she looked at me, frozen with my hand on the doorknob, with large, shocked, cat-like eyes. Her mouth slowly widened in a scream.

"Excuse me."

I stepped back outside and shut the door before she made a sound. Thankfully, I didn't have to hear her scream.

Damn. I should have knocked. Wait, if you're going to change, you could at least lock the door, right?

I was considering whether to transfer the image of her white skin from my retinas to my long-term memory when I heard a timid knock from inside. "Come in," she said in a frail voice.

"I'm sorry."

"No . . ."

I stared at the swirl of hair near the middle of Asahina's head as I apologized. The skin around her eyes became faintly flushed.

"I should apologize for putting you in such embarrassing situations all the time. . . ."

Totally fine with me.

It appeared that she was obediently abiding by Haruhi's request. Asahina had finished changing into the maid outfit and was blushing.

She really is cute.

If my eyes were to meet hers, my brain would be overcome by the images I'd witnessed a moment earlier, and I would really lose it. As I mobilized all of my reason to suppress my libido, I sat down in the brigade chief chair and turned on the computer.

I sensed someone's gaze and looked up to see, oddly enough, Nagato staring at me. She pushed up the bridge of her glasses and returned to her book. Her behavior looked strangely human.

I started up the HTML editor and opened the homepage index file. I was trying to think of something to do with this Web site that still hadn't been updated yet, but I had no idea how or where to start. I just wasted my time as always before closing the file with a sigh. And then I started wondering why I even bothered. Because I was bored and getting pretty sick of Othello.

As I sat groaning with my arms crossed, a teacup was placed before me. Asahina, in her maid outfit, was carrying a tray with a smile on her face. I felt like I was being served by a real maid.

"Thanks."

I had just been treated to coffee by Koizumi, but obviously, I gratefully accepted the tea.

Asahina then gave Nagato her tea and sat down next to her. She blew on the tea to cool it down as she began sipping.

In the end, Haruhi never showed up in the club room that day.

"Why didn't you show up yesterday? Weren't we going to review our behavior on Saturday?"

Same old, same old. I was talking to the occupant of the seat behind me before morning homeroom.

"You sure are annoying. I did the reviewing by myself." Haruhi, sprawled on her desk with her chin propped up, sounded annoyed.

Upon asking, I learned that after school yesterday, Haruhi had gone back over the course her team had taken on Saturday. "I thought we might have missed something."

And here I thought that detectives were the only ones with the habit of repeatedly returning to the scene of the crime.

"It's hot. I'm exhausted. When do we change uniforms? I want to change into the summer uniform as soon as possible."

"We change in June. There's only one week left in May.

"Suzumiya, I've probably said this already, but how about you give up on looking for mysterious things you're not going to find and try having fun the way a normal high-schooler does?"

Her head popped up as she glared at me . . . at least that was how I thought she would react, but contrary to my expectations, Haruhi's cheek remained glued to the desk. She must really be exhausted.

"How does a normal high-schooler have fun?"

Her voice sounded resigned.

"You know. Find some nice guy and conduct your search around town with him. You could even call it a date. Kill two birds with one stone."

I offered this suggestion as I recalled my conversation with Asahina from the other day.

"Besides, you shouldn't have any trouble finding a guy. At least, if you suppress that eccentric personality of yours."

"Hmph. Men are worthless. Feelings of love are just temporary lapses in judgment. Like a kind of mental illness."

She said this lethargically as she rested her head on her desk and stared out the window.

"Even I get in the mood for that stuff every now and then. I am a healthy young girl, after all. My body has its urges. But you know, I'm not stupid enough to let a momentary slip-up leave me saddled with a huge burden. Besides, if I start shopping around for guys, what will happen to the SOS Brigade? I just made it."

Technically, you haven't made it yet.

"You could turn it into some random club that just fools around. You'll get people to join that way."

"No way!"

A curt rejection.

"I made the SOS Brigade because that sort of club wouldn't be any fun. I even recruited an alluring mascot and a mysterious transfer student. Why doesn't anything exciting happen?! Ahh, I need to know if anything crazy is going to happen!"

It was the first time I'd ever seen Haruhi look so defeated, but her crestfallen face was surprisingly cute. She doesn't even need to smile. As long as she has an ordinary expression on her face, she's pretty attractive. Really, it's such a waste.

Afterward, Haruhi spent the majority of morning classes sound asleep. It's a miracle she wasn't caught by any teachers. No, it was just coincidence. Yeah.

However, at the time, some trouble had begun brewing mysteriously in the shadows. It wasn't quite full-blown, so nobody noticed it starting or ending. But at least, as of morning homeroom, it was the only thing I could think about.

Actually, as I was talking to Haruhi that morning, I had a pending issue on my mind. That pending issue would be the note I found in my locker that morning.

There I found . . . AFTER SCHOOL WHEN EVERYONE'S GONE, COME TO CLASSROOM 1-5. . . . in what was obviously a girl's handwriting.

How to interpret this? I had to round up the personalities in my head and hold a conference. Number one was saying, *Something like this has happened before.* But the handwriting was clearly different from Nagato's lettering on the bookmark. The self-proclaimed pseudo-alien had handwriting that was crisp like it was typed. The writing on the note pretty much had high school girl stamped all over it. Besides, Nagato probably wouldn't employ a method as direct as placing a message in my locker.

And so, number two said, *Could it be Asahina?* I also doubted that. I couldn't see her using some ripped-out scrap of paper to call me out without setting a specific time. That's right. Asahina would use an envelope and proper writing stationery. And specifying 1-5, my classroom, as the location would be odd.

Number three went, *What about Haruhi?* Even less likely. She'd just drag me up the stairs to the landing to talk again like that other time. Koizumi was out for similar reasons.

Number four finally said, *Then it's a love letter from some unknown person.* Setting aside the issue of whether or not this was a love letter, it was certainly a piece of correspondence requesting my presence. Though it wasn't necessarily from a girl. Don't let it get to your head. It could just be Taniguchi or Kunikida pulling a prank on me. Indeed. That was the most feasible possibility. This definitely had the markings of a bad joke by that idiot Taniguchi. But if that was the case, I would have expected something more elaborate.

During this sequence of thinking, I paraded around the school interior for no real reason. Haruhi had gone home because she wasn't feeling well. I suppose that was convenient for me.

I made a brief stop in the club room first. If I went back to the classroom too soon, I'd probably get sick of waiting in an empty room for some unknown person. And while I was waiting, Taniguchi might show up saying, "Yo. How long were you waiting? If that little scrap of paper was enough to make you come running, you're pretty naive. Gyahaha." That would be even more aggravating. I'd kill some time, hop over to the classroom, take a peek, make sure no one was there, then head on home. Yeah, the perfect plan.

As I walked along, nodding to myself, I reached the club room. I remembered to knock.

"Yes, come in."

After confirming Asahina's permission, I opened the door. No matter how many times I saw Asahina in her maid outfit, she was still the picture of loveliness.

"You were late today. Where's Suzumiya?"

The sight of Asahina brewing tea is quite becoming.

"She went home. Seemed like she was tired. Now's your chance to counterattack. She's weakened right now."

"I wouldn't do anything like that!"

With Nagato engrossed in reading, sitting in the background, the two of us drank our tea across from one another. It felt like we were back to being an aimless not quite student association.

"Koizumi hasn't come yet?"

"Koizumi showed up earlier, but he said that he had to go to work, so he left."

And what kind of work would that be? Well, at least it looks like the person who sent the letter isn't one of the two other people in this room.

Having nothing else to do, Asahina and I exchanged scattered bits of conversation as we played Othello. After I racked up three wins, we went on the Internet and surfed around news sites until Nagato closed her book with a thump. That had become the signal for us to get ready to go home. I seriously had no idea what the club was doing anymore.

Asahina said, "I'm going to change, so you can go home first." So I took Asahina up on her offer and hightailed it out of the club room.

My watch said it was around 5:30. There shouldn't be anyone left in the classroom.

Even Taniguchi would have gotten sick of waiting and gone home by this point. Regardless, I raced up the stairs past the second floor, heading for the top floor. There's always a slim chance of something happening there. Right?

I took a deep breath as I stood in the empty hallway. The windows were made of frosted glass so I couldn't see inside. All I could see was that the sunset has stained the room orange. I slid open the door to 1-5 nonchalantly.

I wasn't particularly surprised by the fact that someone was inside, but truth be told, I was considerably astonished when I saw the person standing there. Someone completely unexpected stood before the blackboard.

"You're late."

Ryoko Asakura smiled at me.

With a flick of her long, clean hair, she stepped away from the podium. My eyes were particularly drawn to her slender, creamy legs and the white socks extending from below her pleated skirt.

After walking halfway across the room, Asakura, still smiling, turned and beckoned to me.

"Why don't you come in?"

I had been frozen with my hand still on the door. Seeing her motion in my direction, I walked towards her.

"It's you, huh?"

"Yes. Didn't expect me, did you?"

Asakura smiled without a care. The right side of her body was tinted red from the setting sun.

"What do you want with me?"

I purposely asked this in a blunt manner. Asakura chuckled before replying.

"There is something I need you for. I want to ask you something."

Asakura's pale face appeared directly in front of me.

"You know, humans always say, 'It's better to regret something you did than to regret something you didn't do.' What's your opinion on that?"

"I don't know about it being a common saying, but it probably means what it says."

"Then, hypothetically speaking, if there were a situation where maintaining the status quo would only make things worse, but nobody knew what course of action would improve circumstances, what would you do?"

"Come again? Are you talking about the Japanese economy?"

Asakura, still smiling, ignored my question.

"Wouldn't you think that change, any change at all, would be best for now? Nothing will improve the way things currently are."

"Well, I guess that's one way to look at it."

"Right?"

Asakura, arms behind her back, leaned forward a bit.

"But you know, the higher-ups are all stick-in-the-muds who can't keep up with sudden change. But I can't afford such complacency out in the field. A lack of action would only allow the situation to grow worse. In that case, it should be OK for me to act on my own accord to assert changes, right?"

What is she trying to say? Is this a prank? I looked across the classroom, wondering if Taniguchi was hiding in the broom closet. The only other place to hide would be under the teacher's desk.

"I've grown quite tired of observing a static subject. So . . ."

Busily glancing around, I didn't really hear what Asakura was saying.

"I'll kill you and see how Haruhi Suzumiya responds."

There was no time to look confused. Asakura's hand came from behind her back in a flash and a dull metallic light slashed through where my head had been a moment ago.

Asakura smiled like a cat being patted in someone's lap. She held a knife in her right hand over her head. It looked like one of those frightening knives used by the military.

Dodging that first strike was pretty much luck. I was now helplessly sitting on the ground and looking up at Asakura with a dumb look on my face. If I let her get on top of me, I wouldn't be able to escape. I hurriedly leaped up like a grasshopper.

For some reason, Asakura didn't give chase.

. . . No, wait. What's going on here? Why is Asakura trying to stab me with a knife? Hold on a sec. What did Asakura say? Kill me? Why? For what reason?

"Stop joking around."

I was only able to say clichéd phrases in this situation.

"That's really dangerous! A fake knife would be enough to scare anyone, so stop!"

I have no idea what's going on anymore. If somebody does, come here and fill me in.

"You think that this is a joke?"

Asakura asked this with a cheerful expression on her face. She looked anything but serious. Though I suppose a high school girl wielding a knife with a smile on her face is scary enough as it is. Come to think of it, I'm really scared right now.

"Hmm . . ."

Asakura tapped the dull edge of the knife against her shoulder.

"You don't want to die? You don't want to be killed? I really don't understand the concept of death for organic life forms."

This is a joke, right? It wouldn't be too funny if it was serious though. Besides, I was finding this hard to believe. It's not like she was some girl whose reputation I dragged through the mud or had some ugly break-up with. This was the diligent class president I'd barely ever talked to that was trying to slash me with a piece of military-grade cutlery. I couldn't possibly believe she was serious.

However, if that knife was real, and I hadn't made that timely dodge, I would definitely be lying in a pool of my own blood.

"I don't get it. It's not funny. Just put that dangerous thing down."

She paused to think. "Sorry, that's impossible."

A picture of innocence, Asakura smiled the same smile she had when she was with the other girls in the classroom.

"Because I truly want you to die."

She lowered the knife to waist level before charging toward me. Fast! But this time, I was ready. Before she made her move, I shot off at lightning speed to escape from the room — except I crashed into a wall.

?????

There was no door. There were no windows. The classroom wall facing the hallway had become something resembling a gray plaster wall.

Unbelievable.

"It's no use."

The voice drew closer behind me.

"This space is now under my data jurisdiction. Escape routes have been blocked. It was trivial to do. The structures on this planet can be altered with some slight tweaking to the data for molecular bonds. The classroom is now sealed. No one can enter or leave."

I looked behind me. Even the sunset was gone. The windows facing the schoolyard had been replaced by a concrete wall. The florescent lights had turned on while I wasn't paying attention and were shining hollow light across the desktops.

You're kidding, right?

Asakura slowly walked toward me, her faint shadow trailing across the floor.

"Come on, just give up. The result will be the same in the end."

"Who are you?"

I kept looking to make sure, but there was only wall to be seen. No sliding door that didn't quite close. No frosted glass windows. Nothing at all. Or maybe the problem here was with my head.

I gradually wove through the desks, trying to put some distance between she and myself, but she continued to head straight for me. Desks flew out of her way as Asakura walked toward me

unhindered. In contrast, every path I took was blocked by a mass of desks.

This cat and mouse game didn't last long. I suddenly found myself cornered against the end of the classroom.

In that case . . .

I picked up a chair and threw it as hard as I could. The chair changed directions right before it hit Asakura and flew to the side before landing. You've gotta be kidding me.

"It's no use. Didn't I tell you? Right now, everything in this classroom moves according to my will."

Wait. Wait. Wait. Wait.

What? What is this? If this wasn't a joke, and neither Asakura nor I had gone crazy, then what was going on?

I'll kill you and see how Haruhi Suzumiya responds.

Haruhi again? You sure are popular, Haruhi.

"I should have done this from the beginning."

With those words, I became aware of the fact that I couldn't move my body. You can do that? I cry foul play.

My legs were rooted like a tree to the floor without the slightest movement. I couldn't lift my arms. It was like they'd been hardened by paraffin. Actually, I couldn't even move a finger. Frozen in a downward position, I could only watch as Asakura's shoes entered the top of my field of vision.

"If you die, Suzumiya is certain to take some sort of action. I'll probably be able to observe a considerable explosion of data. A golden opportunity."

I don't care.

"Now die."

I sense Asakura raising her knife. What will she aim for? My carotid artery? My heart? If I knew where she would aim, I could at least ready myself. At least I could close my eyes . . . or not. What a riot.

I felt the rush of air. The knife descended toward me.

That was when it happened.

The sound of the ceiling collapsing accompanied a mound of rubble falling down. Fragments of concrete fell on my head. That hurt, damn it! The pouring shower of white stone coated my body. With this much of it, Asakura should also be covered. But when I moved to check, my body wouldn't . . . Huh? I can move now.

I raised my head to look. What did I see?

The point of the knife was almost touching the back of my neck. The expression of surprise was stuck on Asakura's face as she stood frozen, gripping the knife underhand. And there was a small figure of a person holding the blade of the knife with her bare hand — her bare hand, man! — Yuki Nagato.

"Your individual programs were too weak."

That was Nagato in her usual expressionless tone.

"The spatial lockdown and data blockade in the ceiling sector were too weak. That is why I was able to detect you. Why intrusion was granted."

"You're going to get in my way?"

Asakura was every bit as composed.

"If this human is killed, Haruhi Suzumiya is certain to act. That's the only way to obtain more data."

"You are supposed to be my backup."

Nagato spoke in a flat voice, sounding like she was chanting sutra.

"Independent action has not been authorized. You are supposed to obey me."

"And if I don't want to?"

"I will nullify your data link."

"Go ahead and try. I have the advantage in this place. This classroom is now located within space under my data jurisdiction."

"I am requisitioning the nullification of your data link."

The second that was out of her mouth, the edge of the knife she was holding began to sparkle. It then fell apart into microscopic crystals, the way a sugar cube dissolves in red tea.

"!"

Asakura released the knife and suddenly jumped about five meters back. As I watched her do that, I silently pondered.

Ah, they really aren't human. A rather laid-back realization.

After instantly increasing the distance between her and Nagato, Asakura made a soft landing in the back of the classroom. She was still smiling.

There was a soft distortion in space. That's the only way I can describe it. Asakura, the desks, the ceiling, and the floor all shook and appeared to transfigure like liquid metal. I can't really explain it.

All I knew was that space seemed to be condensing into what resembled a spear. But the second that thought crossed my mind, a number of crystals began exploding before Nagato's outstretched palm. At least, that's all I could see.

In the next instant, explosions of crystallized powder began floating down one after the next. The spears created from frozen space attacked us at imperceptible speeds. I didn't realize that Nagato was intercepting all of them at a similar speed until a while later.

"Stay close."

As Nagato fended off Asakura's attack with one hand, she used the other to pull on my necktie. Nagato leaned down, dragging me with her, and I ended up on my knees, positioned behind her.

"Gah!"

Something I couldn't see flew past my head and smashed the blackboard.

Nagato glanced up. In that instant, icicles shot out of the ceiling and rained down above Asakura. She moved so fast you could only see afterimages. Dozens of icicles were thrust into the ground, forming a forest.

"You can't defeat me while we're in this space," Nagato stated.

Asakura stood still, looking completely composed. She faced

Nagato across a distance of several meters. As for me, sad to say, I was hugging the ground, unable to get up.

Nagato stepped over my head and stood up. It's just like her to have gone overboard and diligently written her name on her shoes. Nagato was muttering something in the tone someone would use when reading a novel aloud. It sounded like this.

"SELECT serial_code FROM database WHERE code=data ORDER BY offensive_data_combat HAVING terminate_mode = 'Personal name: Ryoko Asakura'; Judged to be hostile. Nullifying concerned target's connection to organic life form."

The interior of the classroom could no longer be considered normal space. It was just a swirl of distorted geometric shapes, characters, and patterns dancing together. Looking at it started making me dizzy. The visual effect made me feel like I was riding through a fun house. I felt faint.

"You'll cease functioning before that happens."

I had no idea where Asakura's voice was coming from, since she was hidden somewhere in that colorful mirage.

A whirring sound cut through the air.

Nagato swung her heel into me hard and sent me flying.

"What are you . . ."

. . . doing, was what I was trying to say, but an invisible spear shot past my nose and was swallowed by the floor.

"I wonder how long you can last while protecting that thing. Then how about this?"

The next moment, Nagato was standing in front of me, impaled on a dozen light brown spears.

". . ."

Asakura had attacked both Nagato and me at the same time from multiple directions. While some spears had been crystallized and thus disabled, a few that hadn't been intercepted flew toward me, and Nagato used her own body to protect me. That's how it happened. Of course, at the time, I had no way of knowing that.

Nagato's glasses fell from her face and softly bounced to the floor.

"Nagato!"

"There is no need for you to move," Nagato said softly, after taking one glance at the dense cluster of spears protruding from her chest and abdomen.

A small pool of blood began forming around Nagato's feet.

"I am fine."

No, you don't look fine at all.

Nagato pulled out one of the spears sticking out of her body without batting an eye and dropped it to the floor. The blood-stained spear hit the floor with a muted sound. A few minutes later, it transformed into a desk. So that's what the spear actually was?

"Now that you've suffered so much damage, you won't be able to interfere with other data. I'll end this now."

I could faintly see Asakura hidden on the other side of this shaking space. She was smiling. She silently raised her two arms, if I saw correctly, and her arms, from shoulder to fingertip, became enveloped in a dazzling light that extended two arm lengths. No, not just two arm lengths —

Asakura's arms extended even further, shooting out like wriggling tentacles, and attacked from both left and right. "Die."

Unable to move, Nagato's small body shuddered. . . . Warm, red liquid splashed against my face.

Asakura's left arm thrust through Nagato's right side. Her right arm shot through Nagato's left upper chest. Her arms then exited through Nagato's back before finally burying themselves in the classroom wall.

The blood gushing from Nagato's body flowed down her pale legs to widen the pool of blood.

"Finished," Nagato said softly as she seized a tentacle. Nothing was happening.

"What's finished?" Asakura sounded like she was sure of victory. "The three years of your brief life?"

"No."

Even with all those serious injuries, Nagato sounded like there was nothing wrong at all.

"Commence nullification of data link."

It happened suddenly.

My first thought was that everything in the room was shining. But a second later, it all began crumbling into glittering sand. The desk next to me also disintegrated into a gathering of tiny particles before collapsing.

"Impossible . . ."

Asakura stood showered by a rain of crystal grains. This time, she was the one who appeared shocked.

"You are exceptionally skilled," said Nagato. The spears stuck in her body also turned into sand. "That is why it took so long to force a program into this space. But it is finished now."

"You prepared entropy factors before you infiltrated this space. That would explain why you seemed too weak. You had already expended your offensive data before we began. . . ." Asakura spoke resignedly as she watched her two arms also begin to crystallize. "Ah, what a pity. I suppose I was only ever a backup. And I thought it would be a good chance to end this stasis."

Asakura turned to me. She was back to her classroom face.

"I've lost. Lucky you. You get to live a while longer. But you'd best be careful. As you can see, the Overmind has its dissenting voices. Well, humans are the same way. Another agent from the radical faction may come one day. Or perhaps Nagato's master may switch views."

Asakura was already covered from chest to toe with shining crystals.

"Enjoy your time with Suzumiya until then. Bye."

Asakura disintegrated into a small sandpit without a sound. The grains of crystal grew finer and finer before finally dissolving, eventually becoming invisible to the eye.

As the crystals rained down like rustling fine glass, the female student known as Ryoko Asakura was eradicated from this school.

There was a soft thud. I twisted my head in its direction. Finding that Nagato had collapsed, I hurriedly stood up.

"Hey! Nagato, hang in there! I'll call an ambulance."

"No need."

Nagato's eyes were open and staring at the ceiling.

"My body did not suffer significant injury. This space is what must be normalized first."

The avalanche of sand came to a halt.

"I will remove foreign substances and reconstruct the classroom."

And before my eyes, classroom 1-5 turned back into the familiar 1-5, back the way it was. Yes. Like watching a tape rewind, it reverted back into the usual classroom.

The blackboard, the teacher's desk, and the students' desks were born from the white sand. Everything was arranged the way it had been when I left the room after school. What am I supposed to say after seeing this? If I hadn't seen it happen with my own eyes, I would think that it was just well-made CGI.

Window frames projected from what was only a wall and sections then turned transparent to become glass windows. The setting sun colored Nagato and me a shade of red. Just to make sure, I checked inside my desk. Everything that was supposed to be in there was, just the way I had left it. And all that blood from Nagato that had splattered onto my body had disappeared while I wasn't paying attention. Impressive. This had to be magic.

I knelt down next to Nagato, who was still lying on the floor.

"Are you really OK?"

I had to admit that I couldn't see a single scratch on her. And you would expect her uniform to be riddled with holes after being impaled on all those spears, but there wasn't a single one.

"Processing power was redirected to data manipulation and

transformation. The regeneration of this interface was placed in queue. It is currently running."

"Need help?" I asked.

Unexpectedly, Nagato obediently accepted my outstretched hand. I helped her sit up when . . .

"Ah." Her mouth opened slightly. "I forgot to reconstruct my glasses."

"I'd say you look cuter without them. And I'm not really a glasses man."

"What is a glasses man?"

"Nothing. I'm just babbling."

"I see."

This wasn't the time for idle conversation. I would later regret not leaving the room as soon as possible, even if it meant leaving Nagato behind.

The door noisily slid open.

"For-got my stuff, forgot my stuff —"

The person who entered the room, singing some song he had made up, was Taniguchi of all people.

I doubt Taniguchi expected there to be anyone in the classroom at this hour. When he noticed our presence, he froze in his tracks, which was followed by him opening his mouth wide open like an idiot.

At that moment, I had just begun the process of helping Nagato up. If you looked at that particular still-frame, my position would suggest that I was actually pushing her down.

"My bad."

That was Taniguchi in a serious voice I'd never heard him use before. He then stepped back like a crayfish and ran off without shutting the door. I didn't even get a chance to chase him.

"An interesting person," said Nagato.

I let out a huge sigh.

"What do we do . . . ?"

"Leave it to me." Nagato said this as she rested in my arms, motionless. "I specialize in data manipulation. I have made it so Ryoko Asakura has transferred out of this school."

That's your concern?!

This wasn't the time to be joking around. I suddenly shook in astonishment. Now that I stopped to think about it, I had just gone through an incredible experience, hadn't I? This was no longer about whether or not I believed that wild story, that winding freak-talk of Nagato's the other day. Though I still found it hard to believe. I was about ready to piss my pants during the incident just now. I really thought I was going to die. If Nagato hadn't crashed through the ceiling, Asakura would definitely have sent me to meet my maker. After seeing that distorted classroom, Asakura turning into some kind of monster, and Nagato somehow expressionlessly eradicating her, it had been beaten into my mind that everything was real.

Didn't that mean that I had no choice but to accept that Nagato was genuinely connected to aliens or whatever?

On top of that, I was going to end up constantly involved in crazy events at that rate. As I said in the beginning, I just wanted to be a bystander who gets caught up in strange situations. A supporting role would be good enough. But didn't the current situation make me the main character? I can't deny that I had wanted to be a character in one of those stories where things like aliens show up. But it was different now that I actually was such a character.

I'll be honest; this is a problem.

I wanted to be one of those side characters who merrily offers occasional advice from the sidelines to the guy who has to directly deal with all the trouble. I wanted this crazy situation, where my life had been targeted by a classmate, to stop at once. I was still quite partial to being alive.

I spent a brief period dazed and confused, paralyzed in the red-tinted classroom. All the while supporting Nagato's seemingly weightless body.

This is . . . What is this? What am I supposed to think?

Since I had spaced out for a while, I only now noticed that Nagato had been finished with her regeneration or whatever for quite some time and was currently looking up at me without any expression on her face.

The next day, Ryoko Asakura didn't show up for class.

I suppose that it should have been obvious, but apparently, I was the only one who thought so since homeroom-man Okabe said . . .

"Ah —. This concerns Asakura. Due to her father's work — I also find this rather sudden — she has transferred to another school. I was surprised when I heard this morning. Apparently, they went overseas. Seems like they departed yesterday."

And when that really sketchy-sounding story was delivered during homeroom, it was met with "What —?" and "Why —?" from what were mostly girls in an uproar. The guys were whispering about something with their heads together. Teacher-man Okabe also looked like he was deep in thought. Naturally, one particular girl wasn't going to stay quiet.

A fist struck my back with a thud.

"Kyon. Something's up here."

Haruhi Suzumiya, who had completely bounced back, looked at me with shining eyes.

What do I do? Tell her the truth?

Actually, Asakura was a colleague of Nagato, who was created by this unknown group called the Data Overmind. And I don't really know the details, but they had some kind of falling out over whether or not I should be killed. Why kill me? That had something to do with you, Haruhi, and your data or whatever. In the end, she was turned into sand by Nagato. There you have it.

Like hell I can! It's not like I even want to. I would prefer to think that it was all one massive hallucination.

"First, a mysterious transfer student came. Now we have a girl transferring out for no explicable reason. Something's up here."

Should I praise her for her sharp instincts?

"Didn't he say it was because of her father's work?"

"I don't buy that weak explanation."

"It doesn't matter if you buy it. That's the most popular reason people transfer."

"But it's odd. It's only been one day. Less than a day passed between notice of transfer and moving. What kind of job would that be?"

"Maybe he didn't tell his daughter. . . ."

"That's impossible. This matter needs some investigation."

I abandoned the idea of telling her that her father's job was just an excuse and they were actually making a secret move during the night. I know all too well that it wasn't true.

"The SOS Brigade can't sit idly by while a school mystery is waiting to be solved!"

Give me a break.

Yesterday's events demanded that I make significant changes. After all, I had been witness to actual supernatural phenomena. If I pretend that it hadn't actually happened, that would mean I would have to decide if there was something wrong with either my eyes or my mind. Or perhaps there was something wrong with the world. Or maybe this was all just a really long dream.

And I just couldn't bring myself to believe that the world would be unrealistic.

Man. Don't you think that fifteen years and counting is a bit too early for someone to face a turning point in life?

Why did I, in my first year in high school, have to consider such philosophical questions as to how the world should be? I shouldn't have had to think about these things. I'd like it if you didn't give me more work to do. Since I already had another pending issue to deal with.

CHAPTER 6

The pending issue on my mind was another envelope, just like yesterday, in my locker. What was up with that? Was putting letters in lockers the current fad?

But today's was considerably different. This second note was no scrap of paper from an anonymous sender. A name was written on the back of the envelope that looked like it belonged on the side of a girls' manga. And as long as my eyes weren't mistaken in reading the steady handwriting . . .

MIKURU ASAHINA

. . . was what it said.

I swiftly placed the envelope in my blazer pocket and hopped into a stall in the men's bathroom to open it. Written in the middle of the sheet of stationery adorned with characters out of a girls' manga was . . .

I'LL BE WAITING IN THE CLUB ROOM DURING LUNCH. — MIKURU

After the ordeal I had gone through yesterday, my view of the world and reality had gone through a complete barrel roll and was currently spinning out of control.

I hoped to be spared another life-threatening experience if I went to the club room.

However, I had no choice but to go. The person who sent this was none other than Asahina. While I had no evidence to prove that this letter was actually from her, I didn't doubt its origins for a second. She seemed just like the kind of person to use such a roundabout method, and the picture of her cheerfully writing on a sheet of cute stationery fits perfectly with her image, right? Plus Nagato was always in the club room during lunch. If something happened, she'd take care of it.

Don't call me pathetic. I am just an ordinary male high school student.

Once fourth period ended and break started, I escaped the classroom without even eating my lunch, before Taniguchi, who'd been giving me meaningful looks, could come talk to me, Kunikida could invite me to eat lunch, or Haruhi could bring up going to the faculty office to find out where Asakura had moved. I quickly moved toward the club room.

It was still May, yet it already felt like summer. The sun was cheerfully shooting its energy to Earth, as if its furnaces were burning overtime. At this rate, wouldn't Japan end up being a natural sauna by the time summer came? The elastic band on my underwear was soaked with sweat merely from walking around.

I was in front of the literary club room before three minutes had passed. I figured I'd knock.

"Come in!"

It was indeed Asahina's voice. No doubt about it. I would never mistake someone else's voice for Asahina's. It was really her. Relieved, I walked in.

Nagato wasn't there. In fact, Asahina wasn't even there.

A woman stood leaning against the window facing the courtyard. A figure with long hair wearing a white blouse and black miniskirt. She was wearing visitor slippers on her feet.

Her face lit up upon seeing me as she ran over and took my hands in hers.

"Kyon . . . It's been so long."

It wasn't Asahina. It was someone who looked just like Asahina, though. So much that I had to double-check to make sure I wasn't seeing things. Actually, I didn't see how it could be anyone else.

But it wasn't Asahina. My Asahina wasn't that tall. Her face wasn't so mature. The ballooning of her blouse couldn't have increased in size by thirty percent overnight!

The person smiling as she held my hands in front of her chest looked to be around twenty or so. She came across differently from Asahina the high schooler. Even so, she and Asahina were like two peas in a pod. In every way.

"Uh . . ."

I was suddenly struck by an idea.

"Are you Asahina's . . . sister?"

Her eyes narrowed with amusement and her shoulders began shaking. Even her smile looked amused.

"It's me, silly," she said. "The real Mikuru Asahina. But I'm from a later future than the Mikuru Asahina you're familiar with. . . . I've missed you."

I probably looked like an idiot at this point. Yeah, the most acceptable explanation would be that the woman before me was Asahina after a few years had passed. A perfect beauty I could accept as the future version of Asahina.

"Ah, you don't believe me, do you?" Asahina, dressed like a secretary, said mischievously. "I'll prove it to you."

She suddenly began unbuttoning her blouse. After undoing the second button, she thrust her cleavage at a very confused me. "Look. I have a star-shaped mole here, right? It isn't fake. Want to touch it to make sure?"

There was indeed a mole captivatingly protruding from the upper edge of her left breast. Like a solitary accentuation atop her creamy skin.

"Do you believe me now?"

That wasn't the issue here. I didn't know where Asahina had moles on her body. The only times I'd seen that much of her skin would be when she was dressed up as a bunny girl and when I accidentally walked in on her changing. In either case, I didn't have enough time to make any detailed observations. Once I informed her of my thinking, the charming adult Asahina said, "Huh? But weren't you the one who told me I had a mole here, Kyon? I didn't even notice it myself."

She tilted her head in wonder before opening her eyes wide in astonishment. She then suddenly turned bright red.

"Oh . . . no. It's still . . . Oh, I see. It hasn't happened yet. . . . Oh my, what do I do?" Future Asahina clasped her hands to her cheeks and shook her head, shirt still partially open. "I've made a huge mistake. . . . I'm so sorry! Please forget what I just said!"

Easier said than done. Anyway, could you button up your shirt already? I'm having a hard time figuring out where to look.

"I understand," I said. "I'll believe you for now. I've become a person who's ready to believe anything at this point."

"Huh?"

"No, just talking to myself."

This Asahina of an indiscernible age, hands still pressed to her flaming cheeks, finally noticed how my eyes couldn't help but be drawn to her assets, and hurriedly buttoned up her shirt. She then stood up straight and let out a dry cough.

"Do you really believe that I've come to this time plane from the future?"

"Of course. Wait. Does that mean there are two Asahinas in this period right now?"

"Yes. The past me . . . past from my point of view, is currently having lunch with classmates in the classroom."

"Does that Asahina know that you're here?"

"No. I didn't know at the time. After all, she is my past."

Makes sense.

"I needed to tell you something so I made some unreasonable

requests in order to return to this time. I asked Nagato to leave us alone."

It is Nagato we're talking about here so she probably didn't even blink when she saw this Asahina.

". . . Do you know about Nagato?"

"Sorry. That's classified information. My, I haven't gotten to say that in a long time."

"I just heard it a few days ago."

"That's right," Asahina said as she bopped herself on the head and stuck her tongue out. Now she really did look like Asahina.

But then her face suddenly became serious.

"I can't stay in this time very long. So I'll be brief."

Say whatever you want.

"Do you know who Snow White is?"

I stared at this Asahina who was about the same height as me. Her black eyes were slightly moist.

"Well, yeah. . . ."

"When you find yourself in a harrowing situation, please remember those words."

"You mean the story with seven dwarfs, a witch, and a poisoned apple?"

"Yes. Remember the story of Snow White."

"I was just in a harrowing situation yesterday."

"That's not what I'm talking about. It'll happen . . . Let's see. I can't tell you any specifics, but Suzumiya should be with you when it happens."

Haruhi? And me? Caught up in some trouble together? When? Where?

". . . Suzumiya may not find anything wrong with the situation . . . but for you and for the rest of us, it will be a significant problem."

"I suppose that you can't — give me any more details, can you?"

"I'm sorry. Still, just think of it as a hint. This is all I can do."

Adult Asahina looked on the verge of tears. Yeah, she really was Asahina.

"And that would be Snow White?"

"Yes."

"I'll remember that."

Once I nodded, Asahina said that she still had a little time left and looked fondly around the room. She then tenderly brushed her hand against the maid outfit hanging on the rack.

"I can't believe I was able to wear this. I wouldn't be able to do it now."

"You look like you're dressed up as an office lady right now."

She giggled. "I couldn't wear a uniform, so I tried dressing like a teacher."

Some people just look good no matter what they're wearing. I tried asking, "What other costumes did Haruhi make you wear?"

"That's secret. It's embarrassing. Besides, you'll find out soon enough."

Asahina walked over to me, slippers pitter-patting. Her eyes were oddly moist and her cheeks were still flushed.

"I'll be going now."

Asahina continued to stare at my face, like she had something else to say. Her lips parted as if seeking something. Just as I started wondering if I should kiss her and moved to embrace her — she got away from me.

Asahina twisted around suddenly.

"One last thing. Don't get too close to me."

She sounded like a cricket sighing.

As Asahina ran over to the door, I spoke up. "Please tell me one thing!"

Asahina paused right as she was about to open the door, her back toward me.

"Asahina. How old are you right now?"

Asahina turned around with a flick of her hair. Her smile was so brilliant that any person would fall in love.

"That's classified information."

The door shut. There probably wasn't any point in going after her.

Heh, didn't expect Asahina to turn into such a beauty. Then I remembered the first words she had spoken. "It's been so long." Those words can only mean one thing. That is to say, Asahina hadn't seen me for quite some time.

"I see. Makes sense."

Asahina, being from the future, would have to return to her original time before long. A number of years passed before she saw me again. And that happened just now.

I wonder how much time passed for her. Based on her appearance, I'd say five years . . . no, three years? Girls go through some dramatic changes once they're out of high school. I think of my cousin, a brainy type who didn't stand out much. But the second she entered college, she metamorphosed from a chrysalis into a Monarch butterfly. Come to think of it, I didn't know Asahina's actual age. Though I was pretty sure she wasn't really seventeen.

I'm pretty hungry. I should go back to the classroom.

" . . . "

Nagato entered the room with the usual look of cryopreservation on her face. But she wasn't wearing glasses. In the absence of that glass barrier, her eyes bored directly into me.

"Yo. Did you see someone that looked a lot like Asahina on your way here?"

I was just joking when I said that, but Nagato responded.

"Mikuru Asahina's time-divergent variant. I met her this morning."

I couldn't even hear Nagato's clothes rustle as she sat down in a metal chair and opened up a book on the table.

"She is no longer here. She has vanished from this timespace."

"Could it be that you can also travel through time? And that Overmind thing, too."

"I cannot. But time travel is not very difficult. The humans of this epoch are simply unaware of the process. Time is similar to space. Travel is a simple matter."

"Maybe you can tell me how it's done."

"Words would be insufficient for conveying the concept and you would not understand."

"Oh, really?"

"Really."

"Guess that's settled."

"Settled."

I felt like I was trying in vain to talk to an echo. I once again prepared to head back to the classroom. I wondered if there was still time to eat.

"Nagato, thanks for yesterday."

The unnatural look on her face changed ever so slightly.

"There is no need to thank me. Ryoko Asakura's abnormal behavior was my responsibility. My incompetence."

Forelocks of hair swayed gently.

Did she just lower her head?

"You really do look better without glasses."

There was no reply.

I raced back to the classroom where my lunch awaited, figuring I could eat super fast and at least wolf down a few bites. Unfortunately, I ran into this obstacle known as Haruhi right in front of the classroom and was forced to miss lunch. It must have been fate. I'd already resigned myself to whatever might come.

Apparently, Haruhi had been waiting for me in the hallway. She looked irritated.

"Where did you go?! I waited to eat since I thought you'd be back soon!"

"Could you say that again, except this time sounding like an old friend just pretending to be angry?"

"Stop babbling like an idiot and come with me!"

Haruhi used some judo technique to firmly lock my arm in hers, and I was dragged up to that dimly lit staircase landing.

Anyway, I was hungry.

"I just asked Okabe over in the faculty office. Nobody knew about Asakura transferring until today. First thing this morning, a person claiming to be Asakura's father called and said they had to move abruptly. And guess where to? Canada! Does that even make sense? It sounds so made-up!"

"Really, now?"

"Then I asked for her contact information in Canada. I said I wanted to stay in touch."

You never even held a conversation with her.

"And guess what they said? They didn't even have that information! You would normally leave your new contact information, right? Something has to be up here!"

"How about, no?"

"Since I was there, I asked for Asakura's old address. We'll go check it out after school. We might learn something."

As always, she didn't listen to anyone but herself. Well, I wasn't going to bother stopping her. She was the one wasting her time, not me.

"You're coming with me!"

"Why?"

Haruhi squared her shoulders, took a deep breath like a monster about to breathe fire, and shouted loud enough that people in the hallway could probably hear her.

"And you call yourself a member of the SOS Brigade?!"

In accordance with Haruhi's proclamation, I scampered off with my tail between my legs. I returned to the club room to let Nagato know that Haruhi and I wouldn't be here today, and also to let Asahina and Koizumi know if they stopped by after school. But if I only gave the silent alien the message, it might end up turning into a game of telephone, so I took one of the extra paper flyers and wrote SOS BRIGADE, SELF-ACTIVITY DAY WITH HARUHI in magic marker and stuck it on the door with a thumbtack.

I didn't really give a damn about Koizumi, but I should at least save Asahina the trouble of having to change into her maid outfit.

And as a result, I heard the bell signaling the beginning of fifth period on a completely empty stomach. I ate during the next break, though.

Going home from school with a girl is pretty normal in school drama TV shows and I'd be lying if I said I'd never dreamed about that happening to me. And presently, I was living out my dream. I wonder why I was not the least bit happy about it.

"Did you say something?"

That was Haruhi, walking in long strides with a memo in one hand. I figured she meant "Got a problem?" with that line.

"No, nothing."

We quickly descended the hill and walked along the railroad tracks. A little further and we'd reach Kouyou Park Station.

I had been thinking about how we were getting close to Nagato's apartment when Haruhi actually turned in that direction and stopped in front of a familiar, newly-built condominium.

"It looks like she lived in apartment 505 in this building."

"I see."

"See what?"

"No, nothing. Anyway, how are you planning on getting inside? The front door's locked."

I informed her of the number pad next to the intercom.

"Entering a number should open the door. Do you know the code for that?" I asked.

"No. It'll be a battle of attrition."

Against what?

Never mind. It didn't take very long. A lady apparently on her way out to do some shopping opened the door from the inside. She gave a look of disgust at the two of us trying to look innocent before leaving. Before the door could close, Haruhi slipped the tip of her foot in as a stopper.

She wouldn't be winning any smart criminal awards any time soon.

"Hurry up."

After being dragged in, I stood in the entrance hall. We then got on the elevator that happened to be waiting on the first floor. Normal elevator etiquette would require us to stare silently at the floor number display.

"About Asakura."

Looks like Haruhi doesn't give a damn about etiquette.

"There's something else afoot. Apparently, Asakura didn't come to North High from one of the city middle schools."

Well, I'd assume she didn't.

"I did some snooping and found out that she transferred in from a middle school in the suburbs. Something's definitely up with that. It's not like North High's a good school for getting into college. It's just your typical prefectural high school. Why would she bother coming here?"

"I dunno."

"But her residence is so close to school. And it's a condo. Not just some rented apartment. Great location, too. Must be expensive. Did she commute to middle school in the suburbs from this place?"

"I said I dunno."

"Looks like we'll need to find out when Asakura began living here."

We reached the fifth floor and stood in front of apartment 505 for a while, just staring at the door without saying anything. There may have been a doorplate at one point, but it was gone now, a silent indicator that the place was empty. Haruhi jiggled the knob, but naturally, the door didn't open.

Haruhi stood with her arms crossed, contemplating if there was a way to get inside. I stood next to her, trying to stifle my yawn. This was a waste of time, even for me.

"Let's go to the manager's office," said Haruhi.

"I doubt he'll let you borrow a key."

"Not that. I'm going to ask him when Asakura began living here."

"Learning that information won't accomplish anything. Just give up and go home."

"No, I won't."

We took the elevator back down to the first floor and headed for the manager's office at the side of the entrance hall. There wasn't anyone on the other side of the glass door, but a while after ringing the bell on the wall, a little old man with tufts of white hair slowly stepped out.

Before the old man could say anything, Haruhi declared, "We're friends of a former resident, Ryoko Asakura. She suddenly moved and we don't know how to contact her. Did you happen to hear where she moved to? And I was wondering if you could tell me when Asakura came to this place."

I was marveling at the fact that Haruhi could sound like a normal person as the manager, apparently hard of hearing, kept going, "Eh? Eh?" for a period of time. Haruhi was able to successfully learn that the manager had also been surprised by the Asakuras' sudden move ("I was shocked when I found the room empty when I hadn't seen any movers come by"), that

Asakura moved here three years ago ("I remember since the lovely young lady brought me a box of candy"), and that she hadn't needed a loan, but instead paid a lump sum up front in cash ("I supposed she was filthy rich"). She should become a detective.

The old man looked like he was enjoying this chance to talk with a young girl. "That's right. I saw the young lady a number of times, but I don't recall ever meeting her parents —

"Her name's Ryoko? She was a good-natured, kind girl —

"She could have at least said goodbye. What a pity. By the way, you're a fine-looking girl yourself —"

The old man was apparently running out of things to ramble about. Haruhi must have determined that he didn't have any more information to offer.

"Thank you very much for your help." She delivered an exemplary bow before motioning to me. No need to motion. I was already following Haruhi out of the building.

"Lad. That young lady will definitely grow up to be a beauty. Don't let her get away —"

I really didn't need to hear that parting line from the old guy. Pretty sure Haruhi was also within hearing range. I was nervously awaiting Haruhi's reaction, but she kept on walking without a word. I chose to follow her lead in keeping my mouth shut. A few steps out the entrance we ran into Nagato carrying a convenience store plastic bag and her bookbag. She usually stayed in the club room until the school closed, but if she was here right now, she must have left soon after we did.

"Oh? Do you live here, too? What a coincidence," said Haruhi.

Nagato nodded with her pale complexion. It was obviously not a coincidence.

"Then did you hear anything about Asakura?" Nagato gestured a negative response.

"I see. If you learn anything about Asakura, let me know. Okay?" She motioned an affirmative response.

As I stared at the plastic bag containing canned goods and daily staples, I came to a conscious realization that Nagato ate food after all.

"What happened to your glasses?" asked Haruhi.

Nagato just stared at me without answering the question. She was making me uncomfortable. It looked like Haruhi wasn't expecting an answer anyway. She shrugged her shoulders and started off again without looking back. I waved goodbye to Nagato. As I walked past her, she spoke in a soft voice only I could hear.

"Be careful."

Be careful of what this time? I turned around to ask, but Nagato had already disappeared into the building.

I stayed two or three steps behind Haruhi as we walked along the local railroad tracks with no destination in mind. I was just getting further and further away from home. I tried asking Haruhi where she was going.

"It doesn't matter."

That was her response. I continued staring at the back of her head.

"Can I go home now?"

She stopped so suddenly she almost fell forward. She turned to me with a pale face devoid of emotion, like Nagato's.

"Have you ever realized how insignificant your existence is on this planet?"

What are you talking about?

"I have. It's something I'll never forget."

Haruhi began to speak as we stood on the sidewalk of the small road along the railroad tracks.

"During elementary school, when I was in sixth grade, my whole family went to watch a baseball game at the stadium. I wasn't particularly interested in baseball, but I was shocked once we

got there. There were people everywhere I looked. The ones on the other side of the stadium looked like squirming grains of rice packed together. I wondered if every last person in Japan attended this game. And so, I asked my dad, exactly how many people were in the stadium? His answer was that a sold-out game meant around fifty thousand people. After the game, the path to the train station was flooded with people. The sight stunned me. So many people around me, yet they only made up a fraction of the people in Japan. Once I got home, I got a calculator and did the math. I had learned in social studies that the Japanese population was a hundred million and some. Divide fifty thousand into that and you only get one two-thousandth. I was stunned again. Not only was I just one little person in that sea of people in that stadium, but that sea of people was merely a drop in the ocean. I had thought myself to be a special person up until that point. I enjoyed being with my family, and most of all, I thought that my class in school had the most interesting people in the world. That was when I realized it wasn't like that. The things that happened in what I believed to be the most enjoyable class in the world could be found happening in any school in Japan. Everyone in Japan would find them to be ordinary. Once I realized this, I found that my surroundings were beginning to lose their color. Brush my teeth and go to sleep at night. Wake up and eat breakfast in the morning. People do those things everywhere. When I realized that everyone did all these things on a daily basis, everything started to feel so boring. And if there were so many people in the world, there had to be someone living an interesting life that wasn't ordinary. I was sure of it. Why wasn't that person me? That's all I could think about until I graduated from elementary school. And in the process, I realized something. Nothing fun will happen if you sit around waiting. So I figured I would change myself in middle school. Let the world know that I wasn't a girl content with sitting around and waiting. And I did exactly what I wanted to do. But in the end, nothing ever happened. Before I knew it, I was in high school. I thought something would have changed by now."

Haruhi said this all at once, like a contestant in a speech competition. Once she finished, she stared up at the sky, looking like she regretted saying all that.

A train passed by on the tracks. The roaring noise gave me some time to decide if I should make a witty comment or quote some philosophical anecdote to fill up the silence. I pointlessly watched the train disappear into the distance, leaving behind a Doppler effect.

"I see."

My inability to say anything else made me a bit depressed. Haruhi silently patted down her hair, which had been blown around by the gust from the train.

"I'm going home," she said, and headed back the way we came.

As for me, it would be faster to go home that way, but I got the feeling that Haruhi's back was silently yelling, "Don't follow me!" so until Haruhi was out of sight, I just stood there.

What am I doing?

When I got home, I found Koizumi waiting for me outside.

"Hello."

The way he was smiling already like we'd been friends for ten years was awfully fake. Between the uniform and bookbag, he looked just like a person on his way home from school. He waved familiarly.

"I wanted to fulfill my prior promise. I've been waiting for your return. You were earlier than I expected."

"You sound like you know where I went."

Koizumi had one of those "smiles are free" looks on his face.

"Could I have a bit of your time?" he asked. "There's somewhere I want to take you."

"Suzumiya-related?"

"Suzumiya-related."

I opened the door to my house and dropped my bag in the entrance. My sister happened to be walking by, so I let her know I might be home late. I then went back and joined Koizumi outside, and a few minutes later, I was a passenger in a car.

Koizumi hailed a taxi that just happened to pass by with unbelievably perfect timing. The freak and I got in the car, and it took off east on the highway. The destination Koizumi named was a large city outside the prefecture. I was pretty sure it would have been far cheaper to go by train, but oh well, he was the one paying for it.

"Incidentally, what prior promise were you talking about?"

"You wanted proof that I was an esper, correct? An opportunity has arrived, so I thought you might want to come along."

"Is there a point in traveling so far?"

"Yes. I can only demonstrate my powers as an esper in a certain location, under certain conditions. Our current destination happens to fulfill those conditions."

"Do you still think Haruhi is God or whatever?"

Koizumi, sitting in the back with me, turned my way. "Are you aware of the anthropic principle?"

"Never heard of it."

Koizumi exhaled a chuckle before speaking again. "The condensed version is as follows. 'If something must be true for us, as humans, to exist, then it is true simply because we exist.' That's the theory."

"I have no idea what you're talking about."

"'I observe, therefore the universe exists' would be another way to put it. Basically, humans, the intelligent life forms of this planet, discovered the laws of physics and other physical constants and through those discoveries, became aware for the first time of the existence of a universe bound by those observations. Therefore, if the humans on Earth who observed this universe had not evolved to our current level, there would be no one to make those observations and consequently, the existence of the universe would remain unknown. In other words, it wouldn't matter if the universe existed or not. The existence of humanity permits the existence of the universe. This would be the reasoning from a human basis."

"That's just ridiculous. It doesn't matter if humans are around or not. The universe is the universe."

"Precisely. Which is why the anthropic principle cannot be considered scientific. It is merely speculative theory. However, it brings some interesting facts to our attention."

The taxi stopped at a traffic signal. The driver just looked straight ahead. He didn't pay any attention to us at all.

"Why did the universe happen to be created to accommodate human life? If there were a slight increase or decrease in the gravitational constant, the universe would most likely not have facilitated the development of the sun. Or take Planck's constant or particle-mass ratios. They exist in this world at conditions most suitable for humans. Consequently, this universe is what it is, and humanity is what it is. Don't you find that curious?"

My back was starting to itch. Koizumi sounded like a brochure for one of those new pseudoscience religions.

"Don't worry. I do not believe that an omniscient, omnipotent God created humans. Neither do my colleagues. However, we have our suspicions."

"About what?"

"Perhaps we are just clowns standing on tiptoe at the edge of a cliff?"

I must have had a really weird look on my face. Koizumi chuckled like a rooster with asthma.

"I kid."

"I don't understand a thing you're saying."

I got that out in the open. I didn't have time to waste on little stories that weren't funny. Let me out right now or turn the car around. I'd prefer the latter.

"I brought up the anthropic principle to draw a comparison. I haven't gotten to Suzumiya yet."

"So tell me already. Why do you, Nagato, and Asahina all like Haruhi so much?"

"I believe her to be a charming person. But let's set that aside. Do you remember? I once said that the world may have been created by Suzumiya."

"It annoys the hell out of me, but I guess I still remember."

"She has the ability to realize wishes."

"Don't make that kind of a statement with a straight face."

"I have no choice but to make such a statement. The situation is changing the way Suzumiya wishes."

"Like that's possible."

"Suzumiya is positive that aliens exist. She wished it to be so. That is why Yuki Nagato is here. Similarly, she wished for time travelers to exist. That is why Mikuru Asahina is here. And I am also here for the sole reason that Suzumiya wished it so."

"Like I said. How do you know that?"

"It was three years ago."

Screw three years ago. I'm sick of hearing those words.

"One day, I suddenly became aware of the fact that I possessed certain powers. For some reason, I knew how to use those powers. Other people with the same powers experienced similar awakenings. Furthermore, we also knew that Haruhi Suzumiya was the cause. I cannot explain why. We just ended up with that knowledge."

"Let's say I give you the benefit of doubt. I still don't see how Haruhi can do all that."

"Indeed. We found it hard to believe ourselves. How could a single girl have transformed the world, no, perhaps even created the world? And that girl finds this world to be a boring place. This is a terrifying situation to behold."

"Why?"

"Didn't I tell you? If she is capable of creating this world at will, she could undo the world we know and create her desired world from scratch. That would quite literally be the end of the world. Of course, we have no way of knowing if it has already happened. The world we believe to be unique may actually be the latest in a string of reincarnations."

Like I'm gonna believe that. I said something else out loud, though. "Then reveal your true identity to Haruhi. Once she knows that espers really exist, she'll be ecstatic. She might stop thinking about changing the world."

"That would pose another problem. If Suzumiya believes the existence of espers to be a common occurrence, the world would really end up that way. The laws of physics would be bent. As would the law of conservation of mass and the second law of thermodynamics. The entire universe would erupt into chaos."

"There's something I don't get," I said. "You said that Haruhi wished for aliens, time travelers, and espers, which is why you, Nagato, and Asahina are here."

"Yes."

"Then why hasn't Haruhi noticed yet? You people know it. Even I know it. Isn't that kind of odd?"

"You believe it to be contradictory? The contradiction would be within Suzumiya's heart."

"In English, please."

"To be concise, her desire for the existence of aliens, time travelers, and espers contradicts her common sense, which says they cannot exist. She may be eccentric in her speech and conduct, but she is a normal person with rational reasoning. Her sandstorm-level of energy during middle school has alleviated substantially the past few months. I would have preferred that she continue to calm down, but once she came to this school, a tornado touched down."

"What do you mean?"

"It is your fault." Only his mouth was smiling. "If you hadn't given Suzumiya that strange idea, we would probably still be observing her from afar."

"What did I do?"

"You were the one who gave her the idea to form this questionable club. Your conversation gave her the inspiration to create a club made up of unusual individuals. The responsibility is yours. As a result, low-ranked members from the three forces interested in Suzumiya have gathered together in one group."

"That's a false charge."

One of my weaker denials. Koizumi chuckled.

"Well, that isn't the only reason."

And with that, he stopped talking. Before I could tell him to go on, the driver spoke.

"We're here."

The car stopped and the door opened. Koizumi and I got out into the crowd of people. The taxi driver drove off without collecting the fare, but I wasn't particularly surprised.

If anyone living in this region says they're going out on the town, they probably mean that they're coming here. A typical local urban area you could find anywhere in Japan with department stores and complex structures lined up all around and a jumble of private railway and Japan Railways terminals. The setting sun lit up the pedestrians rushing by the intersection with color. Once the traffic signal turned green, a sea of people so big you had to wonder where they all came from, started walking. The two of us had been let off at the edge of the crossing and we quickly slipped into the crowd.

"It may be a bit late to say this after coming all this way." As we slowly walked across the crossing, Koizumi spoke while looking straight ahead. "You can still back out now."

"Just a bit late, eh?"

Koizumi, walking right next to me, grabbed my hand in his. What are you doing? You're freaking me out.

"I'm sorry, but could you close your eyes for a bit? It won't take long. Just a few seconds."

I dodged some sprinting businessman in a suit who was obviously late to a meeting or something. The walk traffic signal began counting down.

Fine. I complied and closed my eyes. The sound of many footsteps. The roar of car engines. Constant chattering. A tumult of noise.

Koizumi led me by the hand. One step. Two steps. Three steps. Stop.

"That's enough."

I opened my eyes.

The world had turned gray.

It was dark. I unconsciously looked up at the sky. The bright orange sun was nowhere to be found. The sky was covered with dark gray clouds. Were they even clouds? It looked like flat seamless space that stretched on forever. My surroundings were covered in shadows. The gray sky emitted soft phosphorescence in the sun's absence, the only light preventing this world from falling into total darkness.

No one was around.

Aside from Koizumi and me, standing in the middle of the intersection, the crowd of people covering the crosswalk had vanished without a trace. The traffic signal continued counting down in the dim light and had just turned red. Yet not a single car moved. It was so silent you might wonder if the earth had stopped rotating.

"The void within a dimensional fault. A place separated from our world. Closed space."

Koizumi's voice echoed rather loudly through the silent air.

"The middle of this crosswalk happened to be the 'wall' of this closed space. Here, like this."

Koizumi's outstretched arm stopped like it had run into an obstacle. I followed suit. It felt like I was touching chilled winter sky. My hand pressed softly into an elastic, invisible wall but met firm resistance before even making it ten centimeters in.

"Its radius is approximately five kilometers. You cannot gain entry through ordinary, physical measures. One of the powers I possess is the ability to enter this space."

Not a single light was on in any of the buildings protruding from the ground like bamboo shoots, nor in any of the stores in the shopping district. The only artificial light was from the traffic signal and the dimly lit street lights.

"Where is this?"

Maybe I should have asked *what* this is.

Koizumi calmly said he would explain as we walked.

"The details are unclear, but this would be an alternate world slightly off from ours . . . at least, you can think of it as such. A dimensional fault sprung from the place we were just at. We have entered the resulting gap. Right now, everything is happening as normal on the outside. The average person will be unable to stumble into this place . . . most of the time, at least."

We crossed the street. Did Koizumi already know where we were going? He seemed sure of himself.

"Picture a dome-shaped space rising from the ground. We would be within that."

We entered a multipurpose building. Forget people. There wasn't even a speck of dust.

"Closed space occurs in a completely arbitrary fashion. There have been instances where they occurred every other day. There were also times when months went by without incident. Only one thing is certain."

We climbed the stairs. It was really dark. If I hadn't been able to see the faint image of Koizumi walking in front of me, I probably would have tripped over myself.

"This space is created whenever Suzumiya becomes emotionally unstable."

We stepped out onto the roof of the four-story multipurpose building.

"I am able to detect the emergence of closed space. So can my colleagues. The reason we are able to do so is a mystery. But we know the location and time of emergence without knowing why. And the method for entry, as well. I am unable to express this sensation in words."

I placed my hands on the railing of the roof and looked up at the sky. There wasn't even a breeze.

"You brought me all the way here to show me this? It's just an empty place, isn't it?"

"No, the crux of the matter is yet to come. It should begin soon."

Stop acting so superior. But Koizumi just pretended not to see the sour look on my face.

"My powers are not limited to detecting and entering closed space. You could say that I've been granted powers which reflect Suzumiya's rationality. If this world is like a pimple resulting from her unstable state, I would be the medicine that treats it."

"Your metaphors are hard to understand," I replied.

"People often tell me that. In any case, you are quite impressive. Not a hint of surprise after witnessing all this."

I recalled the erased Asakura and the gorgeous Asahina. I'd already been through a lot.

Koizumi abruptly looked up. His eyes gazed beyond my head at some point far off in the distance.

"I see that it has begun. Please look behind you."

I looked.

I could see, standing far in the distance between skyscrapers, a shining blue giant.

It was a head taller than a thirty-story commercial building. It looked like its body was glowing from within. Was its slim, dull cobalt-blue body made from some kind of irradiant substance? It had no distinct outline. And nothing you could consider facial features. The places where eyes and mouth would go appeared darker, but the rest of the face was completely blank.

What is that?

The giant raised and shook one arm like it was waving before bringing it down like a hatchet.

It smashed a nearby building in half as it waved its arm. Debris from the concrete and reinforcing bars fell in slow motion and rained down upon the asphalt below with a thunderous roar.

"We believe this to be the manifestation of Suzumiya's irritation. It seems that when the pent-up negative feelings in her pass a certain point, these giants appear and start wrecking their surroundings to relieve her stress. Of course, we can't allow them to run loose in the real world as it would turn into a huge disaster. That is why closed space is created and the destruction only transpires within. Quite a rational method, don't you think?"

Every time the shining blue giant waved an arm, a building would split in half and collapse. The giant would step forward, crushing what was left of the building. I could hear the dull sound of structures being crushed, but oddly enough, I couldn't hear the footsteps of the giant.

"The laws of physics dictate that the legs of a humanoid of such proportions would be unable to support its own weight. The giant is behaving like it is weightless. Its ability to destroy buildings would suggest that it has mass but it would appear that it is not bound by logic. Mobilizing an army wouldn't be enough to stop it."

"So you just let it rampage around?"

"No. That is why I am here. Please watch."

Koizumi pointed his finger at the giant. I squinted. A number of red dots that hadn't been there before were circling around the creature. Compared to the blue giant, who could probably touch the clouds with its skyscraper-level height, the tiny spherical red lights looked like sesame seeds. I counted up to five of them, but they moved so fast that my eyes couldn't keep up. The red dots, orbiting the giant-like satellites, looked like they were trying to obstruct its path.

"My colleagues. Like myself, they were granted power by Suzumiya. We are giant hunters."

The specks of red light skillfully evaded the waving arms of the blue giant impassively wrecking the city. They then abruptly altered their course and charged at the giant's body, which seemed like it was made of vapor. They easily penetrated it.

But the giant apparently paid no attention to the red spheres flying around its face. It ignored their attacks and, almost dutifully, swung its arm down in a karate chop to smash a department store.

Even when the numerous red lights charged together, the giant didn't even flinch. The red lights were so fast that they resembled a cluster of lasers penetrating the giant's body. From this far away, I had absolutely no idea how much damage it had taken. I didn't see a single hole on its body.

"I must join them."

Koizumi's body began glowing red. This would be what you call an aura of visible light. Koizumi's glowing body was eventually engulfed in a sphere of red light. What was before me was no longer human, just a big ball of light.

This is just ridiculous, man.

The sphere of red light softly floated up. It shook left and right two to three times as if waving, before it took off so fast there weren't even any afterimages and flew straight for the giant.

Since the swarm of red lights Koizumi joined never stood still for a second, I couldn't bring myself to count them, but I doubt their number reached double digits. And their valiant use of their bodies to attack merely served to carry them through and didn't seem to have any actual effect. At least, that's my opinion as an observer. But then, one of the red spheres approached the blue giant's arm, attached itself near the elbow, and circled it once.

And with a whoosh, the giant's arm was severed near its elbow. The arm, now without an owner, fell to the ground. At least that's what I expected, but then the blue light sparkled like a mosaic. The arm began to thin and melted like a snowflake bathing in sunlight. Blue vaporous smoke began slowly dripping from the severed elbow. Was that the giant's blood? The scene had definitely entered the realm of fantasy.

The red spheres switched from head-on to piecemeal attacks. They gathered around the giant the way fleas would swarm around a dog and began hacking away at the blue creature. Red lines slashed across the giant's face as its head slid off. Its shoulders collapsed, and before long, its upper torso turned into some kind of weird-looking lump. The severed parts turned to mosaics before disappearing.

Since the blue light was standing in an area of deserted land without anything serving as cover, I was able to observe the entire sequence of events. Once the giant had lost over half of its body, it broke down. It disintegrated into specks smaller than dust. Only the piles of debris remained.

The red dots circling above waited until they were sure it was over before scattering in all directions. Over half of them immediately disappeared out of sight, but one came flying straight toward me. It made a soft landing on the rooftop, went from police-siren red to a shade more akin to a space heater, and began dimming. Once the glow had vanished, all that remained was Koizumi brushing his hair pompously with a smile on his face.

"Sorry to keep you waiting."

He wasn't even short of breath.

"There is one last sight for you to see."

He pointed to the sky. I wondered what else there could possibly be as I looked up at the dark gray sky, and then I saw it.

There was a crack in the sky near where I had first seen the giant. It looked like a hatching chick trying to break out of its egg. The crack began extending in the shape of a spider web.

"Once the blue monster is defeated, the closed space is destroyed. It's quite the spectacle."

While Koizumi was finishing or not finishing his explanation, the cracks covered the entire world. It looked like someone had covered the sky with a huge metal sieve and forgotten about it. The spaces in between the cracks grew smaller and eventually became little more than black curves.

Crash!

There wasn't an audible sound. But I could feel the sound of glass shattering inside my head. A spot of light appeared at the zenith and instantly began widening in a circle. I thought it was raining light, but I was mistaken. It was more like one of those retractable roofs on a dome stadium opening in mere seconds. Except with the entire stadium opening, not just the roof.

Piercing noise rang through my eardrums, and I reflexively covered my ears. But that was just a hallucination after having spent time in a silent world. It was the sound of the hustle and bustle of everyday life.

The world had regained its former state.

The crumbled skyscrapers, gray sky, and flying red lights were nowhere to be found. The road was covered with cars and people again. The familiar orange light of the sun shone between buildings and cast long shadows on all objects blessed by its warmth.

There was a gentle breeze.

"Do you understand now?" Koizumi asked once we were safely in the taxi, which, with unbelievable timing, had pulled up before us after we left the multipurpose building. The driver looked familiar.

"Nope," I responded. I meant it.

"Thought you would say that," came Koizumi's cheerful response. "Those blue monsters — we call them Celestials — are, as I already mentioned, linked to Suzumiya's emotional state. As are we in the Agency. Only when closed space is created, when Celestials are created, am I able to use my paranormal powers. And those powers can only be used within closed space. For instance, I currently have no power."

I silently stared at the back of the driver's head.

"It is unknown why we are the only ones with such powers, but I would assume that any person would have sufficed. It was like winning the lottery. The probability is extremely low, but someone is bound to win. They just happened to have called my number.

"An unfortunate tale," Koizumi finished with an ironic smile on his face. I kept my mouth shut. I had no idea what I should say.

"We cannot leave the actions of the Celestials unchecked. For the greater the extent of destruction the Celestials wreak, the more closed space will expand. The space you just saw was one of the smaller ones. If we leave it alone, it will continue to expand, eventually covering all of Japan, or even the entire world. And in the end, that gray space will take the place of our world."

I finally opened my mouth. "Why do you know this?"

"As I said, I just ended up with this knowledge. The same goes for everyone in the Agency. One day, we suddenly became aware of the fact that we possessed knowledge concerning Suzumiya, the effect she has on the world, and the strange powers we now possessed. As well as the result of leaving closed space untended. It's only natural to do whatever you can once you've learned the consequences. For if we do not act, the world will surely be destroyed."

"Quite a quandary," Koizumi sighed before falling silent.

We just stared at the roadside through the car windows for the rest of the ride to my house.

The car came to a stop and I got out.

"Please be mindful of any trends in Suzumiya's behavior. Her emotional state has been stable for a while now, but recently, there have been signs of agitation. Today's duties were the first in a long time."

"Even if I'm mindful, what's that going to accomplish?"

"Well, you never know. Personally, I would prefer to leave everything in your hands. There are those among us with complicated intentions." Koizumi said all this with his body sticking out through the half-opened door. He then ducked his head back in the car before I could say anything. The door shut. I dumbly watched the car depart like some legendary ghost taxi. I then went into my house.

CHAPTER 7

A self-proclaimed alien-made, artificial human. A self-proclaimed time traveling girl. A self-proclaimed squad of esper boys. Each one had shown me honest proof of their identity. Apparently the three of them, each for their own reasons, had been focusing on Haruhi Suzumiya. Okay, I could live with that. Or no, like hell I could live with that, but even if I accepted everything that had happened and been said, there was still one thing I just didn't get.

Why me?

According to Koizumi, aliens, time travelers, and the esper boys were swarming around Haruhi because she wished for it to happen.

Then what about me?

Why was I dragged into this bizarre mess? I'm a one hundred percent genuine normal human being. I never once woke up suddenly with memories of a weird past life. I haven't done anything worth putting on a résumé. I don't have any super powers or anything. I'm just an ordinary high school student.

Who came up with this scenario?

Or did someone make me inhale some weird drugs and this

was all a hallucination? Was I just in some tripped-out fantasy? Who was pulling the strings?

Is it you, Haruhi?

Yeah, right.

It's no concern of mine.

Why should I have to worry about this crap? It looked like everything was Haruhi's fault. In that case, she should be the one worrying about this, not me. There was no reason for me to be mixed up in all this. None. Absolutely none at all, I say. I had made up my mind. As for Nagato, Koizumi, and Asahina, if they were going to bother revealing their secrets to me, why not just tell everything directly to Haruhi? Whatever happened to the world afterward would be Haruhi's responsibility. It had nothing to do with me.

Run around all you want. Just don't get me involved.

Summer must have been accelerating its arrival. As I walked up the hill dripping sweat, I took off my blazer to wipe away the perspiration from my brow before undoing my necktie and unbuttoning the top three buttons of my shirt, all at a very slow pace. If it was this hot already, I didn't want to imagine what it'd be like at noon. As I reflected upon the lack of meaning in this trek to school that had evolved into a natural hiking course, someone smacked me on the back.

Don't touch me. It'll make me even hotter. I turned around to find Taniguchi's grinning face.

"Yo!"

Taniguchi, walking next to me, was also drenched in sweat. He sounded quite cheerful as he spouted nonsense. "What a pain. Spent all that time to get my hair just right and now it's soaking wet."

"Taniguchi."

I interrupted him as he began going on about his dog, a subject I couldn't care less about, to voice my query.

"I'm a normal high school student, right?"

"Huh?"

Taniguchi had a forced expression of amusement like he just heard some funny joke for the first time.

"Define normal first. We can talk after that."

I shouldn't have asked him.

"Kidding, kidding. Just a joke. Are you normal? Now look here. A normal high school student wouldn't push down a girl in an empty classroom."

I should have known better, but apparently he hadn't forgotten about that.

"I'm also a man. I have enough judgment and pride to refrain from prying the whole story out of you. But you know, yeah?"

Not a clue.

"How did you get so close all of a sudden? And Yuki Nagato, an A– by my ranking."

She's an A–, huh?

Moving on. . . .

"That was just . . ."

I explained. "The story going through your mind is delusional, and completely misguided. Nagato was the unfortunate victim when her club room was turned into Haruhi's base. She had been troubled by the fact that she was unable to engage in literary club activities so she came to me for help. She wanted to know if there was a way to get Suzumiya to withdraw from the room. I sympathized with her, so I felt I should help out the poor girl. We decided to discuss remedial measures somewhere out of Haruhi's sight, so I had the idea of meeting in the classroom once Haruhi had gone home. Then Nagato's chronic anemia kicked in and she fainted, so I quickly put myself between her and the floor. That's when you happened to barge in, Taniguchi. Indeed, once the truth has been brought to light, it seems like such a trivial thing."

"Liar."

Instantly rejected. Damn it. I figured my assorted mix of truth and fiction had created the perfect story.

"Even if I believe your lies, the fact that an antisocial girl like Yuki Nagato would come to you for help already makes you not normal."

Nagato is that well-known, huh?

"Plus, you're one of Suzumiya's people. If you can be considered a normal high school student, then I'm as normal as a water flea."

Guess I might as well ask.

"Can you use ESP?"

"Huh?"

The dumb look on his face got even dumber. You look like you just found out the beautiful girl you picked up was a solicitor for some dangerous religious group, Taniguchi.

". . . I see. You've finally been infected by Suzumiya's poison. . . . Wasn't very long, but it was nice knowing you. Stay away from me or I'll be infected by Suzumiya."

I shoved Taniguchi, and he sputtered, breaking down into laughter. If he's an esper, I'm the UN Secretary-General.

As we walked across the paved stone between the front gate and the school, I suppose I felt somewhat grateful. At the very least, I forgot about the heat for a while.

Not even Haruhi could bear the heat, apparently. She lay sprawled on her desk looking listlessly at the mountains in the distance.

"Kyon, I'm hot."

"Yeah. So am I."

"Fan me?"

"If I'm going to fan anyone, I'll fan myself. I don't have enough energy to be wasting any on you this early in the morning."

Haruhi leaned forward without any sign of having made that speech yesterday.

"What should we have Mikuru wear next?"

After bunny and maid, the next would be . . . Wait, there's more?

"Kitty ears? A nurse outfit? Or perhaps a queen?"

I pictured Asahina's petite frame dressed in each outfit, cheeks flushed. It made me light-headed. She's so cute.

As I began deliberating the matter, Haruhi narrowed her eyebrows, glared at me, and tucked her hair behind her ear.

"Dumb face."

That was how she labeled how I looked. You're the one who brought up the subject. Well, it's probably an accurate description, so I can't really protest. As she fanned her chest with her book . . .

"Seriously, it's so boring."

Haruhi's mouth looked just like an upside-down V. She looked like a character out of a manga series.

The afternoon gym class from hell, being barbequed in the radiation of the sun, came to an end. With disgruntled mutterings of "Okabe, don't make us run for hours, you idiot!" and other assorted cursing, we headed into classroom 1-6 to change out of our uniforms, now soaked rags. We then returned to classroom 1-5.

The girls had gotten out of gym class early and were already finished changing, but since the last period was homeroom, a few people who had sports team practices right after remained in their gym uniforms. For some reason, Haruhi, who wasn't a member of any such teams, was also wearing her gym uniform.

"Because it's hot."

That's why.

"Who cares. I'll have to change again once I get to the club room anyway. And I'm on cleaning duty this week. It's easier to move in this."

Haruhi rested her oval face in her hands as she stared out the window, following the huge towers of clouds.

"Guess that makes sense," I admitted.

We could go with this for Asahina's next costume. Though it wouldn't really count as a costume.

"You're probably fantasizing about something, right?"

Haruhi glared at me after her disturbingly accurate comment. It was like she could read my mind.

"Don't do anything perverted to Mikuru until I get to the clubroom."

I swallowed my *So it's okay once you're there?* and raised both hands in the air like an outlaw who's got a sheriff pointing a gun at him in some Western.

As always, I waited for a response to my knock before entering the room. The maid sitting in her chair like a Therese doll greeted me with a smile like sunflowers in a grassy field. The sight healed my soul.

Nagato, flipping through a book in her corner, looked like a camellia that had bloomed in the wrong season. Yeah, I don't understand my metaphors anymore either.

"I'll make tea."

Asahina adjusted her headband before flopping in her shoes over to the table covered with junk. She carefully placed tea leaves into the teapot.

I sagged into the brigade chief chair and blissfully watched Asahina prepare tea when I was hit by a sudden thought.

I turned on the computer and waited for the OS to boot up. I watched for the mouse icon to switch from hourglass to pointer. Then I opened the freeware viewer and input the password I set to load the contents of the folder MIKURU. I can understand why the Computer Research Society was in tears when they gave this new machine up. The thumbnails for Asahina's maid outfit image collection loaded instantly.

As I verified that Asahina was still preparing tea with one eye, I enlarged one of the images and zoomed in.

This was when Haruhi forced her into her crouching tiger pose. I checked the edge of her exposed, ample cleavage. There was a black dot on her left mound. I zoomed in again. The dot was rather blurred, but it did indeed look like a star.

"I see. That's what she meant."

"Did you just figure something out?"

I closed the window seconds before she placed the teacup on the table. I don't make mistakes. Asahina stood next to me and looked at the monitor. There was nothing to see.

"Huh? What is this? This MIKURU folder."

Gah! I slipped up.

"Why is my name on here? Hey, hey. What's inside? Show me, show me!"

"Uh, this is just, well . . . Hey, I wonder what this is. I'm sure it's nothing important. Yep, that's it. Nothing at all."

"Sounds like a lie."

Asahina reached for the mouse with a playful smile on her face and leaned over me, trying to grab my right hand. *Not happening, sister.* I grabbed onto the mouse. Asahina's face popped over my shoulder as her soft body pressed into my back. I could feel her sweet breath against my cheek.

"Uh, Asahina. Could you let go. . . ."

"Show me —"

Her upper body was crushing my back as she placed her left hand on my shoulder and reached for the mouse with her right. The sensation I felt was killing me.

Her soft giggling tickled my earlobes. It felt so good that I was about ready to let go of the mouse —

"What are you people doing?"

An icy −273°C voice froze Asahina and me. Haruhi stood in her gym uniform with her bookbag over her shoulder, looking like she'd just caught her dad molesting someone.

Asahina unfroze. She detached herself from my back, maid skirt rustling stiffly, and stepped back with robotic movements.

She plopped into her chair like an ASIMO robot whose batteries are almost dead.

Haruhi made a "hmph" sound before stomping over the desk to glare down at me.

"So maids turn you on?"

"What are you talking about?"

"I'm going to get changed."

Go ahead. I drank the tea Asahina had made and made myself comfortable.

"I said I'm going to get changed."

What about it?

"Get out!"

I was practically kicked out of the room as I fell into the hallway. The door slammed in my face.

"What's with her?"

I didn't even have time to set down the teacup. I tugged at my tea-soaked shirt and leaned back against the door.

Why does something not feel right? Something feels different than usual.

"Oh, I get it."

Haruhi had no qualms about changing in the classroom, yet she chased me out of the room just now. That's what was nagging at me.

Well, now. Did she have a change of heart? Or had she finally grown up and learned what shame is? I wouldn't know since the boys of 1-5 were still in the habit of sprinting out of the room right before gym class. Funny, the person who drilled this habit into us, Asakura, was no longer there.

I placed the teacup on the linoleum floor and sat cross-legged, one leg propped up.

After a short while, the rummaging sounds from within the club room ceased without any voice telling me to go in. I hugged my knees and waited ten minutes, then knocked.

"Come in. . . ."

I heard Asahina's small voice through the door. I look past Asahina, opening the door for me like a real maid, to see Haruhi, looking bored, elbows propped on the table, and her long, pale legs. On her head were swaying bunny ears. The familiar sight of her as a bunny girl. Maybe she didn't feel like putting in the effort. Collar and cuffs were absent. Her bare legs weren't covered in fishnet stockings. But the bunny ears were still there as Haruhi sat with her legs crossed.

"My arms and shoulders feel cool, but this outfit doesn't allow much ventilation," Haruhi said as she sipped her tea. Nagato flipped another page.

Surrounded by a bunny girl and a maid, I was at a loss as to how to act. I considered how much I would make if I introduced these two to a part-time job for attracting customers.

"Whoa, what's going on?"

That was Koizumi's merry response in a somewhat hysterical voice, all while maintaining a smile on his face.

"Oh? Was today a costume party? Forgive me. I didn't prepare anything."

Don't say anything that'll make this situation more complicated.

"Mikuru, sit down here."

Haruhi pointed to the metal chair before her. Asahina was obviously cowering as she timidly sat down in the chair with her back to Haruhi. I was wondering what Haruhi was planning when she took Asahina's chestnut hair in her hands from behind and began braiding it.

If you just looked at this scene by itself, it was like a beautiful picture of an older sister arranging her younger sister's hair, but Asahina's face was frozen in fear and Haruhi had a sour look on her face. She probably just wanted to turn her into a maid with braids.

I turned to Koizumi, chuckling deeply as he watched, and asked, "Up for a game of Othello?"

"Sounds fabulous. We haven't played in a while."

We spent the next period of time engaged in the struggle between black and white (Koizumi sucked pretty bad for someone who could turn into a ball of light) while Haruhi braided and unbraided Asahina's hair, then played around by tying it into two pigtails and then a bun (Asahina would shudder every time Haruhi touched her). Nagato was absorbed in her reading and didn't look up for a second.

Why are we all gathered here? It was becoming harder and harder to understand.

That day, we simply engaged in monotonous SOS Brigade club activities. No aliens talking about some space-distorting data. No visitors from the future. No blue giants. No red spheres. Nothing at all. We didn't know what we wanted to do. We didn't know what we should do. We just let the clock tick by as we lived a routine sort of high school life. The everyday happenings of a natural world.

While I did feel a bit dissatisfied when nothing was going on, I could just tell myself, "Oh, well. There's still plenty of time," and aimlessly look to the next day and repeat.

I was still having more than enough fun though. We gathered in the room with no purpose in mind. I would watch Asahina hard at work like a maid. Watch Nagato be as still as a statue of Buddha. Watch Koizumi's perfectly harmless smile. Watch Haruhi's face jump constantly between good and bad moods. All these things had their own sort of essence of the unordinary. And it was part of this oddly satisfying school life I was living. As for almost getting killed by a classmate and encountering some rampaging monster in a gray, uninhabited world, those things just don't happen that often. Though I couldn't write them off as hallucinations, hypnosis, or daydreams.

I did resent being addressed as one of Haruhi Suzumiya's lackeys, but I was the only one lucky enough to be involved, in various ways, with such an interesting group of people. For now, I'd just put aside the question of why I was the only one. Another human may join one of these days.

That's right: I wanted everything to stay this way.

Just about anyone would agree with me on that point, right? Normally, yes.

But there was one person who didn't.

You know who — Haruhi Suzumiya.

Once night had fallen, I had dinner, took a bath, and randomly studied whichever words might come up in English tomorrow. Once that was finished, the clock indicated that it was time to sleep. As I lay down in my bed, I perused the novel Nagato had forced on me. I figured a little reading was good every now and then, so I opened up the book. It was unexpectedly engaging as I continued reading page after page. I guess you really can't judge a book by its cover.

But it was a bit too long for me to finish in one night, so I put down the book once one of the characters finished a long monologue. The demons of sleep were setting up camp on my eyelids. I marked my spot with the bookmark Nagato had written on and shut the book. I then turned off the lights and sank under the covers. Within a few minutes, I was sound asleep.

Incidentally, do you know why people dream? Sleep rotates between cycles of REM and non-REM stages. The first few hours of sleep are deep sleep and spent mostly in non-REM sleep. The brain is in a restive state during this stage. Once the body is resting and the brain becomes semi-active, you're in REM sleep. This is when we dream. The closer we get to morning, the higher the frequency of REM sleep. Which means that most of our dreams last until right before we wake up. I dream every night, but I lie in bed until the last possible second so once I wake up, I have to frantically get ready for school and end up forgetting what my dream was about. Though on occasion I abruptly recall some dream I'd forgotten about years ago. Yeah, human memory is still an unsolved mystery.

But I digress. None of that really matters.

Someone was slapping my cheek. You're annoying. I'm sleeping. Don't interrupt me when I'm comfortably asleep.

". . . Kyon."

My alarm clock hadn't gone off yet, even though I just turn it off every time it does. I should still have some time before my mother sends my sister to merrily drag me out of my bed.

"Wake up."

No. I want to sleep. No time for dubious dreams.

"I told you to wake your ass up!"

The hands wrapped around my neck began shaking my head. When the back of my head slammed against a hard surface, I finally woke up.

. . . Hard surface?

I quickly sat up. Haruhi's face, which had been staring at me, dodged my head.

"Finally awake?"

Kneeling next to me in her sailor uniform was Haruhi. Her pale face was filled with anxiety.

"Do you know where we are?"

Yeah. School. The school we go to, North Prefectural High. The paved stone between the front gate and the lockers. Not a single light was on. At night, the school building looked like a gray silhouette to my eyes —

Hold on. . . . There was no night sky.

Just a flat plane of dark gray. A monochrome sky emitting soft phosphorescence. No moon, stars, or clouds. A gray sky that resembled a wall.

Closed space.

I slowly stood up. I wasn't wearing my sweats that served as pajamas. Instead, I was clothed in my school uniform.

"I thought I had woken up, but then I found myself here, and you were lying down next to me. What's going on? Why are we at school?" Haruhi asked in an unusually subdued voice.

Instead of responding, I groped around my surroundings. Both pinching the back of my hand and touching my uniform felt far too real for this to be a dream.

"Haruhi, are we the only ones here?"

"Yeah. I know I was sleeping in my bed, so how did I end up here? And the sky looks strange. . . ."

"Did you see Koizumi?"

"No . . . Why?"

"No reason. Just asking."

If this is that dimensional fault or closed space or whatever, then the giants of light and Koizumi and his buddies should also be here.

"Let's leave the school grounds for now. We might run into someone somewhere."

"You don't seem very surprised."

I'm surprised. Especially by the fact that you're here. Wasn't this a playground for those giants she created? Or was this just an unusually real dream I was having? Alone with Haruhi in a deserted school. I wonder what Freud would have to say about this.

I maintained a reasonable distance from Haruhi as we stepped through the gate when my nose ran into an invisible wall. I remembered this clammy sensation. I could force my way a bit further but I soon ran into firm wall. An invisible wall stood right outside the school entrance.

"What is this?"

As Haruhi vigorously pushed with her two hands, her eyes grew wider. I walked around the school premises to confirm my suspicions. An imperceptible wall extended seamlessly as far as I could walk.

Almost as if it were trying to trap us inside.

"It doesn't look like we can get out from here."

There wasn't even a breeze. The air was totally still.

"Let's try circling to the back."

"Shouldn't we try to contact someone first?" Haruhi asked. "If there's a phone, at least. I don't have my cell on me."

If we were in closed space, then according to Koizumi's explanation, a phone wouldn't do us any good, but we still went into the school building. There should be a phone in the faculty office.

None of the lights were on. The dark school building was pretty creepy. We walked past the rows of lockers and headed into the silent school building. On the way, I flipped the light switches in the first-floor classrooms and the fluorescent lights flickered on. It was just cold, artificial light, but it was enough to make the two of us exchange relieved looks.

First, we headed for the night watchman's office. After confirming that it was empty, we headed for the faculty office. Naturally, it was locked, so we pulled out a nearby fire extinguisher, smashed its bottom into the glass window, and broke into the room.

Haruhi held the phone out to me. "Doesn't seem to work." I took it and put it to my ear. No sound at all. I tried pushing the buttons a few times but nothing happened.

We left the faculty office and headed up, turning on all the lights in the classrooms as we went. Our classroom was on the top floor. If we looked down from there, we might learn something about our surroundings. At least that's what Haruhi said.

As we walked through the school, Haruhi tightly clenched the sleeve of my blazer. "Don't expect much from me, Haruhi. I don't have the power to do anything. But if you're scared, just cling to my arm. It creates more of an atmosphere."

"Idiot."

Haruhi glared at me with upturned eyes, but her fingers didn't release their grip.

Nothing looked different about classroom 1-5. Looked just the way it did when I left it that afternoon. The eraser marks on the chalkboard. The thumbtack-filled mortar wall.

"Kyon, look. . . ." Haruhi said after rushing over to the window before falling silent. I stood next to her and looked down at the world below.

The gray world extended as far as I could see. Our school was built on the side of a mountain so you could see the shoreline from the fourth floor. I looked 180 degrees to the left, then 180 degrees to the right. Everywhere I looked, I saw no light suggesting human life. All the houses were plunged in darkness. Even the ones covered by curtains didn't have any light spilling out. As though every last person had vanished from this world.

"Where are we . . . ?"

It wasn't that everyone else had disappeared. We were the ones who had disappeared. In this case, we would be the intruders who had slipped into this deserted world.

"This gives me the creeps," Haruhi murmured as she hugged her shoulders.

We didn't know where to go. And so we made our way to the club room we had just left that evening. We had swiped the key from the faculty office, so we had no trouble getting in.

Under the fluorescent lights, we sighed with relief at returning to our familiar headquarters.

I turned on the radio but there wasn't even any white noise. Without the slightest hint of wind, the only sound in the club room was the sound of me pouring water into the teapot. I didn't feel like bothering to change the tea leaves, so it was just diluted tea. I'm the one who brewed it. Haruhi was just half-dazed, staring at the gray world outside.

"Want tea?"

"No."

I carried my teacup and pulled out a metal chair. I took a sip. Asahina's tea is a hundred times better.

"What's going on? What is this? I don't get it. Where are we? Why am I in this place?" Haruhi said all this without turning around, still standing at the window. From behind, she looked really thin. "And why is it just you and me?"

"Hell if I know." Haruhi flipped her skirt and hair and looked at me with a pissed-off look on her face.

"I'm going to go explore a bit," she said as she headed out of the room. I began to stand up.

"You stay here. I'll be right back."

And with that, she left the room. Hmm, I guess that's typical of her. As her lively footsteps faded into the distance, I sipped my unsavory tea. That was when he finally showed up.

A small red ball of light. At first, it was the size of a ping pong ball. Then its outline gradually grew in size while flickering like a firefly before settling into the shape of a human.

"Koizumi?"

Though it had a human shape, it did not look human. No eyes, nose, or mouth. Just a shining red doll.

"Why, hello."

An optimistic voice broadcasted from within the red light.

"Took you long enough. I was expecting you to appear in a more tangible form."

"Regarding that, I need to tell you a few things. No beating around the bush. I'll be frank. This is an abnormal situation."

The red light flickered.

"With normal closed space, I am easily able to gain entry. However, that wasn't the case this time. I could only appear in this incomplete form after borrowing the power of all of my colleagues. And it probably won't last very long. The power that rests within us is beginning to disappear."

"What's going on? Are Haruhi and I the only ones here?"

"Precisely," Koizumi responded. "In other words, what we

feared has already begun to happen. Suzumiya has finally given up on the current world and decided to create a new world."

". . ."

"As a result, our superiors are in a state of panic. Nobody knows what will happen to our world once it has lost its God. If Suzumiya happens to be feeling merciful, our world may continue to exist without change. But it could also return to nothing in the next second."

"Why did this happen?"

"No one knows."

The red light faltered like a flame.

"In any case, you and Suzumiya have completely vanished from our world. You are not in ordinary closed space. It is an entirely new dimension created by Suzumiya. Perhaps all the previous instances of closed space were merely practice runs."

"Funny joke. Tell me which part I'm supposed to laugh at. Ha. Ha. Ha."

"That wasn't a joke. I am dead serious. The world you are in is probably the manifestation nearest to the world Haruhi desires. Though we aren't sure what it is that she wants. Indeed, who knows what will happen?"

"Setting that aside, why am I here?"

"Do you really not know? You have been chosen by Suzumiya. The only person from the old world Suzumiya truly wanted to be with. I thought that you had realized this long ago."

Koizumi's light was about as dim as a flashlight running out of batteries.

"It would appear that I'm almost out of time. The way things look now, I probably won't be seeing you again, but I suppose I'm rather relieved, for I will no longer need to go hunt Celestials."

"Do I have to live in this gray world all alone with Haruhi?"

"Adam and Eve. If you reproduce enough, it'll work out, won't it?"

". . . Don't make me hit you."

"Just a joke. All kidding aside, I would assume that this closed area of space will only last momentarily. It should soon turn into a familiar-looking world. However, it probably won't be entirely the same. You could say that the world you are in is now the real world and the former world would be closed space. It's a pity I won't be able to observe the differences between the worlds. Well, if I happen to be born into the new world, please treat me kindly."

Koizumi was turning back into a ping pong ball. His human shape collapsed and shrank like a burned-out star.

"We can no longer go back to the old world?"

"If Suzumiya desires it, then perhaps. The possibility is slim though. As for myself, I would have liked to spend more time with you and Suzumiya, so I regret this turn of events. I enjoyed being in the SOS Brigade. Oh, that's right. I forgot to deliver the messages from Mikuru Asahina and Yuki Nagato."

Koizumi said the following words before completely disappearing:

"Mikuru Asahina wanted to apologize. She said, 'I'm sorry. It's all my fault.' Yuki Nagato's message was 'Turn on the computer.' I'll be going now."

The end was quite quick. Like a candle being blown out.

I pondered Asahina's message. Why is she sorry? What did Asahina do? I decided to think about that later and turned on the computer per the other message. As the hard drive produced sounds of seeking, the OS logo showed up on the monitor . . . except not. The OS screen, which should have booted up in a few seconds, didn't show up. The monitor remained black. There was only a blinking white cursor on the left edge of the screen. The cursor began moving soundlessly to spell out a curt message.

YUKI.N> Can you see this?

After a brief period of bewilderment, I pulled the keyboard towards me. My fingers began typing.

Yeah.

YUKI.N> The connection has not been completely severed with your spacetime. But it is only a matter of time. The connection will be closed soon. That will be the end.

What should I do?

YUKI.N> Nothing can be done. The eruption of abnormal data in this world has completely vanished. The Data Overmind is in despair. The possibility for evolution has been lost.

What was that whole possibility of evolution thing anyway? What part of Haruhi could possibly be considered evolved?

YUKI.N> A high level of intelligence refers to data processing speed and accuracy. The intelligence of organic life forms has limited processing capabilities due to error and noise data from their physical bodies. As a result, once they reach a certain level, evolution stops.

So our physical bodies are the problem?

YUKI.N> The Data Overmind was created from data to begin with. It was believed that their data processing ability would increase infinitely until the universe burned up. But that was wrong. Just as the universe had its limits, evolution had its limits. At least, as long as they remain a discarnate entity of data.

And Suzumiya?

YUKI.N> Haruhi Suzumiya possessed the ability to create data from nothing. An ability the Data Overmind does not have. A human, a mere organic life form, is creating more data than it can process in its lifetime. If we could analyze this ability to create data, we could find a clue regarding autoevolution, or so we thought.

The cursor flickered. I could feel her hesitance before the words began racing again.

YUKI.N> We are counting on you.

Counting on me?

YUKI.N> We wish for you to return to this world. Haruhi Suzumiya is a vital observation subject. An important being that may never be born into this universe again. I also individually feel that I want you to return.

The letters were fading. The frail cursor slowly produced words.

YUKI.N> Another visit to the library would

The monitor blacked out. Increasing the brightness didn't help. Nagato's final typed words were brief.

YUKI.N> sleeping beauty

The loud rattling of the hard drive scanning almost made me jump up. The access light blinked and the monitor displayed the familiar OS screen. The whirring of the computer fan was the only sound in this world.

"What are you telling me to do, Nagato? Koizumi?"

I let out a deep sigh and casually, really, just casually looked out the window.

The window frame was covered in blue light.

A giant of light stood in the courtyard. Up close, it looked like a blue wall.

Haruhi jumped into the room.

"Kyon! Something's here!"

Haruhi almost ran into me as I stood at the window before coming to a halt next to me.

"What is that? It sure is big. A monster? It isn't a mirage, right?"

She sounded excited. Like her earlier gloom had never happened. Her eyes shone without a hint of anxiety.

"Maybe it's an alien. Or the revival of some super weapon developed by an ancient race! Is that what's keeping us from leaving the school?"

The blue wall stirred. My mind flashed back to the scene of skyscrapers being trampled down. I immediately grabbed Haruhi's hand and ran out of the club room.

"Wha — H-Hey! What are you doing?"

We practically fell into the hallway. At the same time, a large roar vibrated through the air. I pushed Haruhi to the floor and covered her with my body. The clubhouse shook violently. I could hear the sounds of hard, heavy objects crashing into the floor down the hallway. Based on the volume of sound, the giant apparently hadn't targeted the clubhouse with its attack. It was probably the building across the way.

I grabbed Haruhi's hand and pulled her up as she sputtered. I then took off running. Oddly enough, Haruhi followed without complaint.

Is it my palm that's sweating? Or is it Haruhi's?

The taste of dust in the decrepit clubhouse was gone. As I

dashed as fast as I could to the stairs, I heard a second crashing sound.

We raced down the stairs. I could feel Haruhi's body heat through her hand. We cut across the courtyard and headed down the slope to the track. Upon first glance, Haruhi's face next to me looked, though I may be mistaken, somewhat happy. Like a kid on Christmas morning finding all the presents she'd wanted next to her bed.

We kept running to put some distance between us and the building. When I looked up, I became truly aware of how big the giant was. The one in the place Koizumi took me to had been about as big as a skyscraper.

The giant raised its arm and smashed its fist into the school building. The first hit had already split open the cheap four-story structure, so it collapsed rather readily. Debris flew in all directions, causing deafening noise.

We stopped after advancing to the center of the two-hundred-meter track. A gigantic blue humanoid rose against the gloomy monotone canvas like a Hollywood special effect.

I was thinking about how this was what Haruhi should be taking pictures of for our Web site. She didn't need to put up pictures of the Computer Research Society president groping Asahina, much less pictures of her in costumes. This scene is what she should put on the Web site.

As I was thinking about that, the sound of Haruhi rapidly speaking reached my ear.

"Do you think it'll attack us? It's just a hunch, but I don't think it's anything evil."

"Dunno."

As I responded, I was thinking to myself about what Koizumi explained when he first took me into closed space. If we left the destructive actions of the Celestials unchecked, the world would eventually be replaced. As in this gray world would take the place of the former world. And then . . .

What would happen next?

According to Koizumi, a new world was apparently being created by Haruhi. Would the Asahina and Nagato I know be in it? Or would it be a world where abnormal became normal, where these Celestials walked freely and aliens, time travelers, and espers were everywhere?

If that were to happen, what would my role be in that world?

There was no point in thinking about it, since I didn't have a clue. I didn't know what Haruhi was thinking. I'm no master at reading other people's minds. I have no skills at all.

As I stood deep in thought, Haruhi's cheerful voice sounded near my ear.

"What is all this? This weird world and that giant."

It looks like you made them. Both this place and that thing. Anyway, what I want to ask is why I've been dragged into this. Adam and Eve, you say? That's just dumb. I won't accept such a clichéd turn of events. I refuse to.

"Don't you want to go back to our old world?" I asked, sounding like I was reading off a script.

"Huh?"

Haruhi's shining eyes seemed to dim. I turned to her white face juxtaposed against the gray backdrop.

"We can't stay in this place for the rest of our lives. It doesn't look like there's a place to eat when we get hungry. There probably aren't any stores open. And if that invisible wall extends around this entire place, we won't be able to get out. We'll surely starve to death."

"Hmm, you know. It's kind of strange, but I'm not really concerned about any of that. I just get the feeling it'll work itself out. I know something's wrong, but I just, I don't know . . . I'm having fun right now."

"What about the SOS Brigade? It's the club you made. You're just gonna ditch it?"

"That doesn't matter anymore. After all, I'm really enjoying

myself right now. There's no need to go look for anything mysterious anymore."

"I want to go back."

The giant suspended its dismantling of the school.

"I discovered something after being thrown into this situation. I may complain all the time, but I actually liked how my
life was. Including that idiot Taniguchi and Kunikida. Koizumi, Nagato, and Asahina. You can even include the vanished
Asakura."

"What are you talking about?"

"I want to see them again. I feel like I still have so many things
to tell them."

Haruhi's head lowered a bit. "I'm sure we'll see them. This
world won't be covered in darkness forever. The sun will rise
tomorrow. I can tell."

"That's not what I mean. I don't mean in this world. I want to
see the old them in the old world."

"I don't get it."

Haruhi made a pouting face and looked up at me. She had this
strange mixed look of hatred and sorrow like some kid who had
her present taken away.

"Weren't you fed up with that boring world? It was just an ordinary world where nothing special ever happened. Didn't you
want something more interesting to happen?"

"I did indeed."

The giant began walking. It kicked down the wreckage of the
collapsed school building and advanced into the courtyard.
It karate-chopped the passageway between buildings and punched
the clubhouse. Our school was being blown apart. And our
club room.

I looked over Haruhi's head to see the base of more blue walls
standing in different positions from the giant. One, two, three . . .
I stopped counting once I got to five.

The giants, unhindered by the red balls of light, began destroying the gray world as they pleased. It must have been my twisted mind telling me they were probably having a good time doing this. Every time they waved their limbs, the landscape vanished, like a piece of space being shaved off.

Half the school was gone without a trace.

I was unable to sense if the closed space was expanding. Plus I really didn't know anything about the whole "expanding until this space becomes the new reality" thing. I just knew that was how it was. Right then, if a drunk middle-aged guy sitting next to me on the train were to say, "Don't tell anyone, but I'm actually an alien," I probably would have believed him. I already had three times the amount of experience I'd had a month ago.

What can I do? It would have been impossible a month ago, but now, I could do it. I'd already received a few hints.

I resolved myself and spoke.

"Haruhi, I've been through some really fantastic experiences the past few days. You probably don't know, but there are actually a bunch of extraordinary people interested in you. You could even say that the world is revolving around you. These people, they consider you to be a unique girl and are acting accordingly. You may not have realized, but the world was definitely moving in an interesting direction."

I wanted to grab Haruhi's shoulders when I realized I was still holding her hand. Haruhi, however, had a look on her face like she thought I had mad cow disease.

Unconsciously, Haruhi avoided my eyes and watched a giant take apart the school like it was completely natural.

As I looked at her from the side, I become newly aware of the softness of the curves of her face. Nagato said she was the "potential for evolution." According to Asahina, she was a "time warp." Koizumi treated her as "God." Then what about me? What did "Haruhi Suzumiya" mean to me?

Haruhi was Haruhi and nobody else. I wasn't going to use such overblown language to dodge the question. But I didn't happen to have a decisive answer. Isn't that natural? If someone points to the classmate sitting behind you and asks, "What is she to you?" how are you supposed to respond? . . . No, sorry. Guess that's still dodging the question. Haruhi wasn't just a classmate to me. Of course, she also wasn't the "potential for evolution" or a "time warp," much less "God." She couldn't possibly be.

The giant turned toward the track. It has no face or eyes, yet I could feel it looking at us. It began walking. Each step carried it meters. Despite its sluggish movements, the creature's approaching figure loomed before us.

Think. What did Asahina say? Her warning. And Nagato's last message. Snow White. Sleeping Beauty. Even I should know what Sleeping Beauty was referring to. What do the two have in common? The answer became clear once I factored in our current situation. So clichéd. Way too clichéd, Asahina. And Nagato. I wouldn't accept this stupid turn of events. No way in hell.

Or so my rational thought insisted. Nagato might call it "noise." Humans are not rational creatures. I released Haruhi's hand, grabbed the shoulders of her sailor uniform, and turned her toward me.

"What is it?"

"Actually, ponytails turn me on."

"What?"

"That ponytail you used to wear looked so good it was criminal."

"Are you an idiot?"

Her black eyes appeared to reject me. As Haruhi raised her voice in protest, I forced my lips onto hers. It's expected to close your eyes in such situations so I did, which is why I didn't see the expression on Haruhi's face. Maybe her eyes were wide open in shock. Maybe her eyes were closed like mine. Maybe she had her arm raised over her head about to smack me. I have no way of knowing. But I wouldn't have noticed being smacked right then. I'm willing to bet that anyone in this situation with Haruhi would feel the same way. I strengthened my grip on her shoulders. I didn't want to let go just yet.

I could hear roaring sounds in the distance. The giants were probably punching and kicking the school again. But in the next second, a sense of weightlessness threw me off balance. I fell, experiencing an excruciating impact on my left side. My kiss shouldn't have warranted a judo throw. But then I opened my eyes and froze upon seeing a familiar ceiling.

I was in a room. My room. I looked to the side to find my bed and discovered that I had fallen onto the floor. Naturally, I was wearing my sweats. Half of my disheveled blanket had fallen off the bed. My arm was behind my back and my mouth was wide open like an idiot's.

It took a while before I regained my senses.

I stood up half-conscious and pulled open the curtains to look outside. I could see a few stars and street lights shining here and there. Once I saw a flickering light on in one of the houses, I began walking in circles in my room.

A dream? Was it all a dream?

Stuck in a world all alone with a girl I know and I end up kissing her. Freud would have a field day with this. Did I really have a dream that's such an easy read?

Gah, I want to hang myself this very second!

I should probably be grateful that Japan eliminated the right to bear arms. If an automatic handgun had been within my reach, I would have popped myself in the head without hesitation. If it had been Asahina, I could have picked at my honest desires within the dream. But it was Haruhi, of all people. What the hell was my subconscious thinking about?

I sat wearily on my bed and threw my arms over my head. If it

was a dream, it was the most realistic one I'd ever had. My right hand was covered in sweat and I could still feel a warm sensation on my lips.

. . . Or this was no longer the old world. It was the new world Haruhi had created. If that was the case, was there a way for me to confirm that?

No. Maybe, but I couldn't think of anything. Actually, I didn't want to think at all. If I was going to have to accept that my brain was capable of coming up with such a stupid dream, I'd rather the world be destroyed. It made me want to pull my hair out.

I picked up my alarm clock and checked the time. 2:30 AM.

. . . I'm going back to bed.

I pulled my covers over my head and attempted to coax my frozen brain into slumber.

Only I didn't sleep a wink.

Which is why I walked up the hill to school the next day in a foul mood. Quite frankly, it was painful. The only saving grace was that I didn't run into Taniguchi and have to deal with his stupid blabbering. The blazing sun faithfully engaged in full power nuclear fusion. Would it kill the sun to lower the thermostat every now and then for our sake?

The sleepytime fairies, which hadn't shown up when I wanted them to, were now circling over my head. I really doubted I'd hear much, if any, of what was said in first period.

Once the school was in sight, I stopped and stared bemusedly at the decrepit four-story building. The front gate, clubhouse, and passageway, sucking in students the way an anthill sucks in ants, were all there. I dragged my legs slowly up the stairs to head for my familiar 1-5 classroom. I stopped moving three steps from the open doorway.

Haruhi was already sitting in the last row next to the window.

Why? She had her chin in her hands as she looked out the window. The back of her head was in plain sight.

A tied-off portion of her black hair stuck out like a topknot. It wasn't really a ponytail. She just tied off a bit of hair, didn't she? Still . . .

"Yo. How's it going?" I asked.

I dropped my bag on my desk.

"I feel miserable. I had a nightmare last night," Haruhi answered in a flat voice.

Well, isn't that a coincidence.

"I ended up not getting any sleep. I've never wanted to skip school as badly as I do today."

"Oh, really?"

I sat down in the hard chair and peered at Haruhi's face. The strands of hair above her ear were covering the side of her face, so I couldn't really make out her expression. Just as well. I could tell she wasn't in a good mood. At least, that's the impression I got.

"Haruhi," I said.

"What?"

As Haruhi refused to budge from staring out the window, I said to her, "Your hair looks nice today."

EPILOGUE

Let's talk a little about what happened afterward.

By noon, Haruhi had untied her hair and restored it to its former straight style. She probably got sick of that knot. Once her hair grows longer, I'll try indirectly suggesting she try a ponytail again.

I ran into Koizumi during break, on the way back from the restroom.

"I need to thank you," he said with an overly easy smile on his face.

"The world remains unchanged. Suzumiya is still here. It looks like I won't be out of a job just yet. Indeed, you did really well. I'm not being sarcastic. Although we can't discount the possibility that this world was newly created last night. In any case, I feel privileged to see you and Suzumiya again."

He said that this might be the beginning of a long friendship as he waved goodbye.

"I'll see you after school."

When I went to the club room during lunch, I found the usual sight of Nagato reading.

"You and Haruhi Suzumiya disappeared from this world for two and a half hours," were the first words out of her mouth. And the only words. As Nagato began to ignore me like I was a stranger and silently read, I opened my mouth.

"I'm reading the book you lent me. I can probably return it in another week or so."

"I see."

As always, she didn't look at me.

"Tell me. How many others like you are on Earth?"

"Many."

"Will another one like Asakura attack me?"

"Don't worry."

For once, Nagato raised her head and looked into my eyes. "I won't let them."

I decided not to mention what I had thought of her at the library.

After school, Asahina was, oddly enough, wearing her sailor uniform instead of her maid outfit in the club room. When she saw me, she threw her body onto mine.

"I'm so glad to see you again," Asahina said in a tearful voice as she buried her face in my chest. "I thought you'd never — *sniff* — be able — *sniff* — to return to this world —"

Maybe she felt my arms creeping around behind her. Asahina suddenly thrust her arms into my chest and pushed me away.

"We . . . we mustn't. If Suzumiya sees us like this, it'll happen all over again."

"I don't understand what you mean."

Her large, teary eyes were beyond lovely. You could be born anew looking at them. No man in the world could resist her eyes of pristine innocence.

"You're not going to wear your maid outfit today?"

"It's being cleaned."

That's when I remembered. I pointed to a spot above my heart.

"I just remembered something, Asahina. You have a star-shaped mole around this spot on your chest, right?"

Asahina wiped the tears from the corner of her eyes and made a face like a passenger pigeon after a shotgun was fired right before its eyes. She quickly turned around and tugged the neckline of her dress to look down her chest. Her ears instantly turned red, which amused me to no end.

"H-how did you know?! I never knew it was shaped like a star! Wh-wh-wh-wh-when did you see it?!"

Even Asahina's neck was turning red as she hit me with her fists like a child.

Should I tell her the truth? Your future self told me.

"What are you people doing?" Haruhi queried from the doorway, disgusted. Asahina's clenched fist froze as her face became pale again. But Haruhi lifted the paper bag she was carrying with a wicked grin on her face, like an evil stepmother who had just heard that her stepdaughter had eaten the poisoned apple and died.

"Mikuru, you're probably sick of the maid outfit, right? Come on. It's time to change."

Like a master of ancient martial arts, Haruhi crossed the gap in an instant and captured the stiffened Asahina without any trouble at all.

"No — Ah — Wha — St-sto —"

As Asahina screamed, her uniform was forcefully removed.

"Stop struggling. Resistance is futile. This time, you'll be a nurse. A nurse! Or do they say hospital attendant these days? It doesn't matter. It means the same thing."

"At least close the door!"

I would have liked to stay and watch, but I excused myself from the room, shut the door, and clasped my hands in prayer.

Of course, during this entire sequence, Nagato had been sitting at the table reading her book.

The paperwork for chartering the SOS Brigade had been sitting on the shelf for quite some time, but just now, I finally turned in to the student council a document that vaguely resembled an application. The "Save the World by Overloading it with Fun Haruhi Suzumiya Brigade" would definitely be rejected unless I bribed them, so I arbitrarily changed the name to the "Support the Student Body by Overworking to Make the World a Better Place Student Service Brigade (Student Association)" (a.k.a. SOS Brigade). I listed the club activities as "counseling in regards to school life, consulting services, and participation in local volunteer activities." I didn't really know what that all meant, but if the application ended up being accepted, I could stick up a poster on the bulletin board offering counseling. I doubted our counseling would help anyone, though.

Meanwhile, under Haruhi's supervision, the city-wide "magical mystery patrol" was still going strong. Today we commemorated its second occasion. As always, the plan would be to waste an entire day, but by pure coincidence, Asahina, Nagato, and Koizumi were all unable to go. They mentioned something about important tasks they couldn't get out of. And so, I was now waiting for Haruhi by myself next to the station's ticket gate.

I didn't know if the three of them were just trying to give us some space, or if some emergency had actually cropped up. However, since the three of them were anything but ordinary people, it was quite possible that they had to deal with some funny business that was going down right then in some unknown place.

I checked my watch. I still had thirty minutes until we were supposed to meet. I'd already been standing there for thirty minutes, as I had arrived an hour early. It's not that I was particularly eager to get cracking, but there was the whole SOS Brigade practice of fining the person who arrives last, regardless of whether that person's late or not. And there were only two people today.

When I looked up from my watch, I immediately saw a familiar, casually clothed figure in the distance. She probably didn't expect to find me waiting for her thirty minutes early, seeing as she froze in her tracks before indignantly stomping toward me again. I didn't know if the creased brow and scowl on her face were lamenting today's low attendance or lamenting her failure in arriving after me. I would have plenty of time to ask about it later while Haruhi treated me to a drink at the café.

In fact, I had a number of things I wanted to talk to her about. Like what kind of activities Haruhi had planned for the SOS Brigade. The costumes I'd like to see Asahina in. That she should talk to other classmates besides me. Her opinion on Freud and dream interpretation. And so on and so forth.

But when it came down to it, I already knew what I was going to tell her first.

I was planning on telling her about aliens, time travelers, and espers.

AFTERWORD

For one reason or another, I have this belief that the amount of writing a person is capable of in a lifetime is decided from birth. Assuming that there is a predetermined set amount of words, then the more you write, the more that amount will depreciate. That would forecast the eventual loss of your ability to write. In practical application, let's say someone wanted to fill up 300 pages of paper with 400 words crammed onto each sheet in one day. Since there's no precedent of that ever happening, I may actually be right. Of course, if I did want to write 120,000 words in one day, the fact that typing at the speed of one word per second would already take thirty-three hours would mean I could never do it. But there might be someone out there who can accomplish the feat, so I can't be totally sure.

Speaking of things I can't do, I'll change the subject to how cats are nice. They're cute and soft and they meow. You're probably wondering where I'm going with this. I don't really know myself. Not sure how to explain it. I'll be quite happy if you can accept the "it is what it is" explanation.

Incidentally, I believe that this book was only able to see the light of day after receiving the incredible and very appreciated Sneaker Award. When I was informed that I had won the prize,

I was questioning my ears, then my mind, the telephone, reality, and whether or not the earth was rotating. Eventually, the thought *it's apparently true* crossed my mind, so I began dancing around swinging my cat for no real reason, when it suddenly bit me. I remember that as I stared at the scratches on my palm, I thought that if humans had a predetermined set amount of luck, then I had already used up all of mine. I don't remember much of what happened after that. After all, the shock to my mind created some gaps in my memory, so I can't be sure. Though I get the feeling that a lot happened.

Which is why I concluded that the effort put in by the people who had to do all the work and make decisions to get this book published was probably over twice that of the actual author. If I were to attempt to express the gratitude I feel right now, I would probably be unable to find the words to convey how thankful I am. I am especially at a loss for how to show my appreciation to the members of the selection committee. In fact, I'm in the process of devising a new expression, but since it would be my own creation, it would probably end up being interpreted as nonsense. In any case, I am truly grateful. Thank you very much. From the bottom of my heart. I truly mean it.

Right now, I feel like I'm standing at the starting line, not knowing if I'll trip when the starting shot is fired and not knowing which direction the finish line is. I might be on a track without any water stops. Even if I stray off the path, I just deeply hope that I can keep on running. Except this isn't the time for me to be talking about this stuff like it doesn't concern me.

To wrap things up, I would like to express my boundless gratitude to all the people of the publishing company who were directly or indirectly involved and all the people who read this book. That's all for now.

Nagaru Tanigawa

THE MELANCHOLY OF
HARUHI SUZUMIYA

……WHAT?
I HAVE NO INTEREST IN ORDINARY HUMANS.
IF THERE ARE ANY ALIENS, TIME TRAVELERS, SLIDERS,

OR ESPERS HERE...
...COME JOIN ME.
THAT IS ALL.

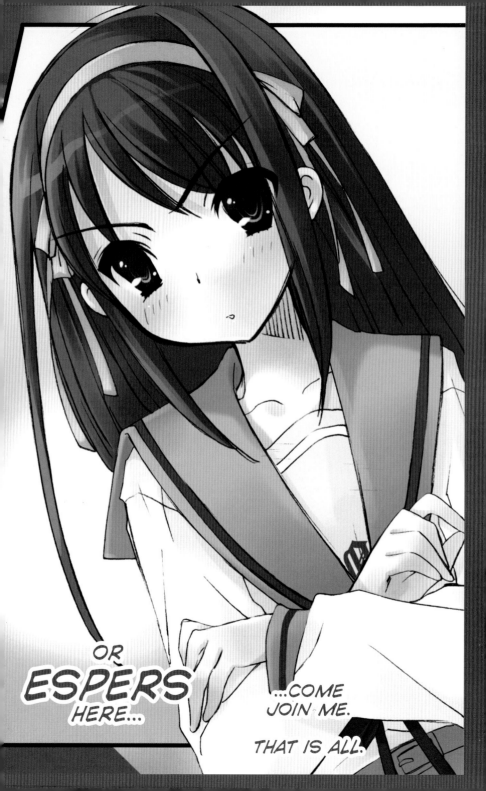

YUKI NAGATO CONTINUED READING HER BOOK AS THOUGH NOTHING WAS HAPPENING. IT'S A PEACEFUL WORLD, IN A WAY.
NOOOOOOOOOOOO!
STOOOOOOOOOOP!!

C'MON! CHANGE INTO THE BUNNY-GIRL OUTFIT ALREADY!

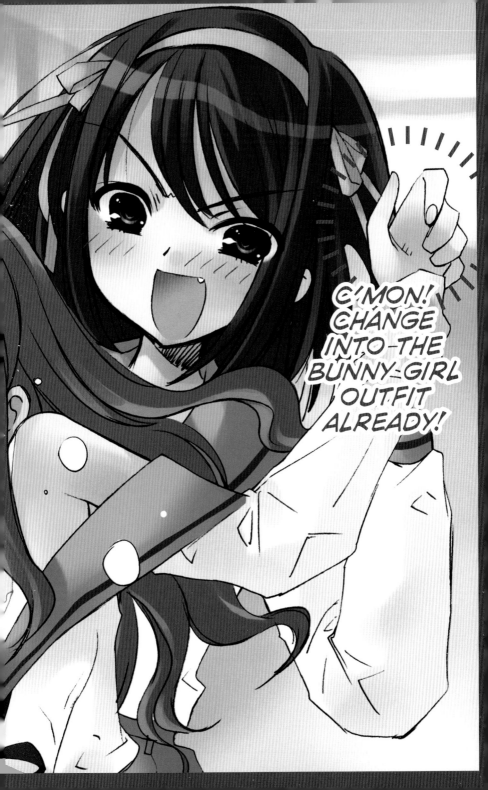

HEY, KYON.
WHAT IS THAT GIANT?

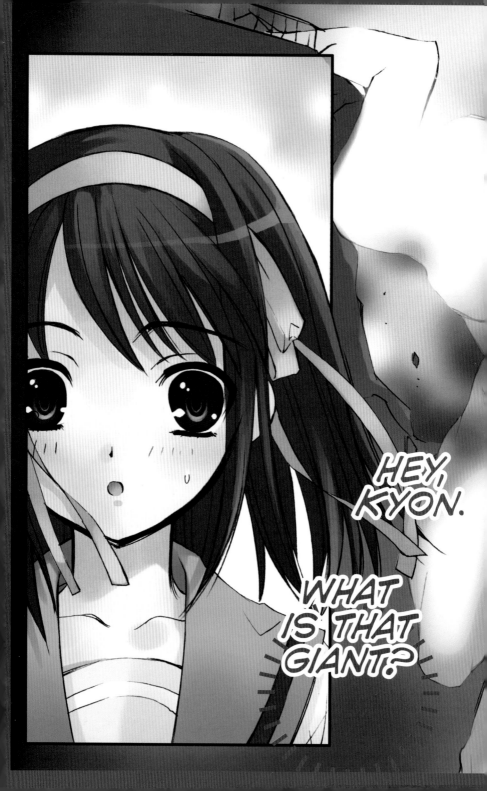

THE BLUE LIGHT ROSE UP AND BEGAN DESTROYING THE SCHOOL BUILDING.

OH!
FLIP THE BOOK OVER FOR A PREVIEW OF THE MELANCHOLY OF HARUHI SUZUMIYA THE MANGA!

CHECK OUT A PREVIEW OF THE MANGA ADAPTATION OF

THE MELANCHOLY of HARUHI SUZUMIYA

Nagaru Tanigawa's *The Melancholy of Haruhi Suzumiya* has been such a phenomenon in Japan that it spawned both an animation and manga adaptation. Please flip your book over to the "back" to enjoy a preview of the manga version of *The Melancholy of Haruhi Suzumiya* currently in stores!

If you're not already familiar with manga, it's worth pointing out that Japanese reads right to left so you should move through the panels and pages in "reverse" order.

THE MELANCHOLY OF HARUHI SUZUMIYA
①

Original Story: Nagaru Tanigawa
Manga: Gaku Tsugano
Character Design: Noizi Ito

Translation: Christine Schilling
Lettering: Alexis Eckerman

SUZUMIYA HARUHI NO YUUTSU Volume 1 © Nagaru TANIGAWA • Noizi ITO 2006 © Gaku TSUGANO 2006. First published in Japan in 2006 by KADOKAWA SHOTEN PUBLISHING CO., LTD., Tokyo. English translation rights arranged with KADOKAWA SHOTEN PUBLISHING CO., LTD., Tokyo through TUTTLE-MORI AGENCY, INC., Tokyo.

English translation © 2008 by Hachette Book Group, Inc.

Yen Press
Hachette Book Group
237 Park Avenue, New York, NY 10017

Visit our Web sites at www.HachetteBookGroup.com and www.YenPress.com.

Yen Press is an imprint of Hachette Book Group, Inc. The Yen Press name and logo are trademarks of Hachette Book Group, Inc.

First Yen Press Edition: October 2008

ISBN: 978-0-7595-2944-1

10 9 8 7 6 5 4 3 2 1

Printed in the United States of America

I'M SUCH A ROMANTICIST.

YEAH, RIGHT.

IN ANY CASE...IT'S UNDENIABLE THAT THERE'S A PART OF ME THAT'S JEALOUS OF SUZUMIYA'S APPROACH TO LIFE.

AFTER ALL, SHE'S WAITING FOR THE DAY SHE'LL RUN INTO THE EXTRAORDINARY, WHILE I'VE LONG SINCE GIVEN UP ON THAT.

...WOULD BE ONE OF TRAGEDY AS SHE LOOKED OFF SOMEWHERE DEEP IN THOUGHT.

THAT'S NOT HOW IT IS...

IN THE BACK OF MY MIND, AN IMAGE OF HARUHI SUZUMIYA DRAWING A WHITE LINE ON THE PITCH-BLACK CAMPUS WITH HER SERIOUS EXPRESSION POPPED UP.

SMEARING THE GROUND WITH THE LIME SHE'D SWIPED FROM THE SHED AHEAD OF TIME...

...HER EXPRESSION ILLUMINATED BY THE FAINT LIGHT...

RYOUKO ASAKURA!
CLASS PRESIDENT!!
SHE'S A GIRL WHO STANDS OUT IN A COMPLETELY DIFFERENT WAY FROM SUZUMIYA!
FIRST OFF, SHE'S A TOTAL BABE!
CAN YOU HELP US WITH THIS...?
QUIET AND LEVEL-HEADED—THE WORKS!
YOU SUBSTITUTE THIS IN, AND THEN...
THIS GOES THIS WAY...
OOH! I GET IT NOW!
THANKS, CLASS PRESIDENT!
WAAAI (YAAY)
SHE'S AT THE TOP OF HER STUDIES, AND POPULAR WITH THE OTHER GIRLS TOO.
IN SHORT, AN AAA RANK!!
BUT...
...DESPITE ALL THAT, YOU'RE STILL AIMING FOR SUZUMIYA, EH?
HAA (SIGH)
GOOD LUCK.
WH-

THERE WERE THESE GINORMOUS, BIZARRE CHARACTERS ON THE SCHOOL GROUNDS...

...THAT SHE SCRIBBLED OUT ALL BY HERSELF AFTER SNEAKING INTO THE SCHOOL IN THE DEAD OF NIGHT.

DON'T TELL ME THE FIVE MINUTE RELATIONSHIP SHE HAD WAS WITH HIM...

DABA (FLAIL)

W-WE WENT TO THE SAME MIDDLE SCHOOL...

DABA

DABA

HOW DO YOU KNOW SO MUCH ABOUT SUZUMIYA?

URK!!

WAI (GAB)

WHETHER THEY WERE PART OF A CEREMONY TO SUMMON DEMONS OR A MESSAGE TO UFOS... THE DETAILS REMAIN A MYSTERY TO THIS DAY.

EVEN WHEN QUESTIONED ABOUT IT, SHE REFUSED TO COMMENT.

WAI

WAI

THE GIRL THAT'S REALLY IN SEASON IS...

IN ANY CASE, JUST GIVE UP ON SUZUMIYA.

FOR A WHILE THERE, SHE WAS HOPPING FROM ONE GUY TO THE NEXT. BUT AS FAR AS I KNOW...

...THE LONGEST RELATIONSHIP SHE'S HAD LASTED A WEEK, AND THE SHORTEST WAS FIVE MINUTES.

WITHOUT EXCEPTION, SUZUMIYA'S ALWAYS THE ONE TO CUT IT OFF.

KATA (CLATTER)

AND SHE ALWAYS GIVES THE SAME EXCUSE.

I DON'T HAVE TIME TO WASTE WITH ORDINARY HUMANS.

YOU'VE SEEN HER ECCENTRIC BEHAVIOR ALREADY, HAVEN'T YOU?

...THE HEADLINE DURING MIDDLE SCHOOL: "PRANK GRAFFITI ON SCHOOL CAMPUS"!

SHE'S ABNORMAL... THE INCIDENT THAT BACKS IT UP MOST CONCRETELY WAS...

PERFECT TIMING.
THERE'S SOMETHING I WANTED TO WARN YOU ABOUT AS A FRIEND.
IF YOU'VE GOT YOUR EYE ON SUZUMIYA, YOU'RE BETTER OFF GIVING IT UP.
WHAT!?
DID YOU THINK YOU COULD FOOL ME? I WENT TO MIDDLE SCHOOL WITH HER.
I KNOW YOU'RE WATCHING HER OUT OF THE CORNER OF YOUR EYE, RIGHT?
WH-
JUST QUIT WHILE YOU'RE AHEAD. SHE'S WAY OUT OF YOUR LEAGUE.
YOU KNOW, DON'T YOU? HOW ALL THE GUYS DIG HER.
YOU CAN'T DENY SHE'S GOOD-LOOKING. NOT TO MENTION SHE EXCELS AT EVERY SPORT AND HAS TOP GRADES.
YOU COULD CATEGORIZE HER AT AN A+ RANK.

ZAWA
(MURMUR)

...THERE WASN'T A PERSON LEFT AT SCHOOL WHO DIDN'T KNOW HARUHI SUZUMIYA'S NAME.

OH, IF IT ISN'T TANIGUCHI AND KUNIKIDA.

MORNING.

QUIT CALLING ME BY THAT NICKNAME ALREADY...

MORNING, KYON!

ぱっ
PA (GLOW)
U-UM, YOU'VE GOT A GREAT BODY, SUZUMIYA-SAN!
YEAH, YOU DO! I'M SO JEALOUS!
YOU ON A DIET OR SOMETHING?
ばん
BAN (SLAM)
THAT'S NONE OF YOUR BUSINESS.
う
URK...
がたん…
GATAN (CLATTER)
W-WELL... WE SHOULD GET GOING...
ふんっ
HMPH!
SO SHE'S WEARING HER HAIR DIFFERENTLY AGAIN TODAY, EH?
BEFORE EVEN A WEEK HAD PASSED SINCE HER SURPRISE ATTACK SELF INTRODUCTION...

HEY, DID YOU CATCH THAT SHOW YESTERDAY?

OH, YOU MEAN THE ONE THAT STARTS AT 9 O'CLOCK?

I'M NOT WATCHING THAT ONE.

...I WANTED IT TO BE A COINCIDENCE.

THE SERIES SO FAR WENT LIKE THIS—

YOU SHOULD WATCH IT SOME TIME, SUZUMIYA-SAN.

IT'S SO GOOD!

"UGLY CAT-LOVER"

A ROMANCTIC SITCOM ABOUT UGLY CATS!

OOOOOO

NOT INTER-ESTED.

GIRO
(GLARE)
I WAS AWARE JUST HOW BADLY...

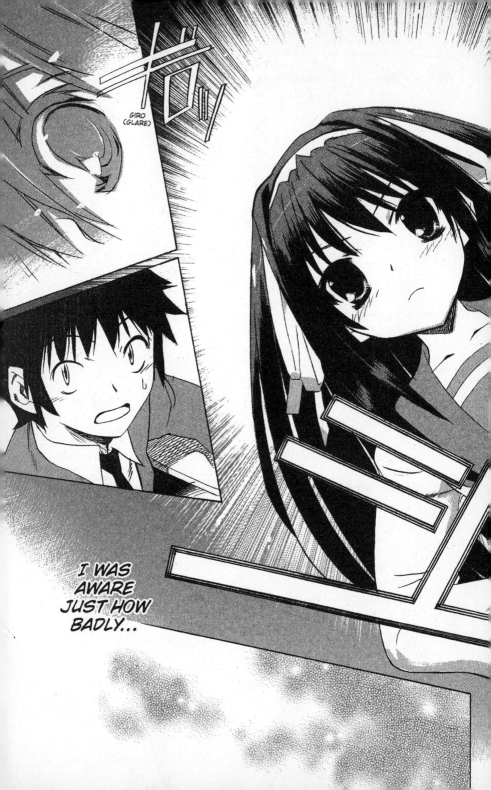

DON (BAM)
THAT WAS HOW WE MET.

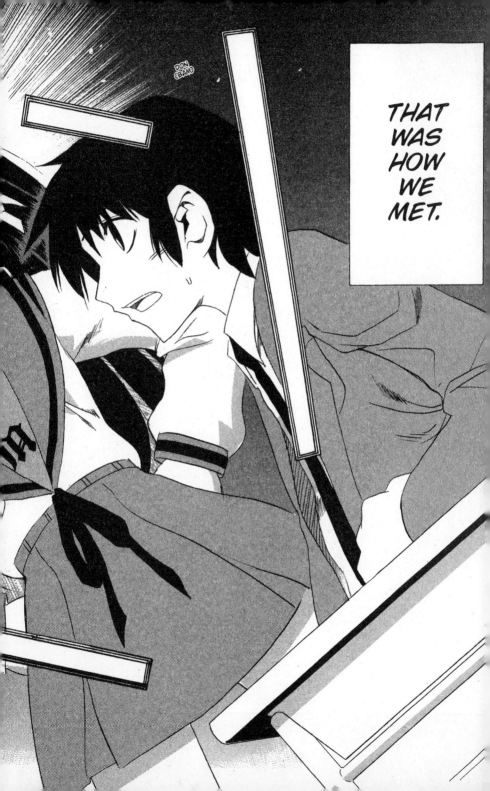

IT'S NOT THAT I'VE GOT NO EXPECTATIONS FOR MY NEW LIFE, BUT...
...WITH THE MAJORITY OF MY CLASSMATES COMING FROM THE SAME MIDDLE SCHOOL, FOR BETTER OR FOR WORSE, IT WAS A STABLE BEGINNING.
...OR SO I THOUGHT.
NAILED IT!
GATAN (CLATTER)
HARUHI SUZUMIYA FROM HIGASHI MIDDLE SCHOOL.
IF THERE ARE ANY ALIENS, TIME TRAVELERS, SLIDERS, OR PSYCHICS HERE, THEN COME JOIN ME.
THAT IS ALL!
BOY, I'LL PROBABLY NEVER FORGET THIS FOR THE REST OF MY LIFE.

IN ANY CASE, STARTING THIS SPRING, I'M A HIGH SCHOOL STUDENT JUST LIKE ANY OTHER.
1-5
OKAY, THEN...
...TO START ON THE RIGHT FOOT OF YOUR NEW LIVES...
BOARD: SELF INTRODUCTIONS
...LET'S HEAR EVERYONE'S INTRODUCTIONS FOR THE FIRST DAY.
I'M TANIGUCHI FROM HIGASHI MIDDLE SCHOOL, AND...
DOKI
DOKI (BADMP)
DOKI
ALL RIGHT. NEXT, PLEASE.
YES, SIR!

HEROES IN ANIME AND SANTA CLAUS...
...ONLY EXIST IN DREAMS.
I MUST HAVE ALREADY REALIZED THAT.
ONLY I DIDN'T WANT TO ACCEPT IT.
...RIGHT?
BECAUSE WHETHER A DREAM OR NOT...
...THE ME BACK THEN WAS COMPLETELY ENTHRALLED BY THEM.
...AS IF.
SOS